©Noboru Kannatuki
AF575521
4
GOBLIN SLAYER

And he must never be defeated.

He lets no preparation go undone.
It is not only his sword, armor, shield, and helmet;
he neglects none of his many items.
Of course, simply because precautions have been taken
does not mean one will be triumphant.
But one will not be defeated
because one was unprepared.
©Noboru Kannatuki

High Elf Archer
Guild Girl

Cow Girl
Priestess

"What do you mean, who?"

"I mean which girl, dumbass… Other than Guild Girl!"

"This again? Keep watching for enemies, you two. They'll come from above. Be careful."

"We know, already. Why do you think we're going through all these cliffs and forests?"

"Fine, then…"

"I bet I can guess your type. You like the stiff, serious girls, don't you? They'd sure make a good match."

"Aw, shaddup. Listen to you talk—and here you're in a party with that gorgeous woman."

"What do you know? If a woman understands what a guy's worth is, it'd practically be rude not to chat her up! So? What's your answer?"

"…I'm not particularly interested."

"You're kidding. Wait. Don't tell me… you're into m—"

"No."

"...It seems they are not goblins."
"...Well, that's what's important. So who *is* your main squeeze?"

Contents

GOBLIN SLAYER

Volume 4

KUMO KAGYU

Illustration by
NOBORU KANNATUKI

New York

GOBLIN SLAYER

KUMO KAGYU

Translation by Kevin Steinbach ✣ Cover art by Noboru Kannatuki

Original Japanese edition published in 2017 by SB Creative Corp.
This English edition is published by arrangement with SB Creative Corp., Tokyo, in care of Tuttle-Mori Agency, Inc., Tokyo.

Yen On
150 West 30th Street, 19th Floor
New York, NY 10001

Visit us at yenpress.com ✣ facebook.com/yenpress ✣ twitter.com/yenpress
yenpress.tumblr.com ✣ instagram.com/yenpress

First Yen On Edition: December 2017

Yen On is an imprint of Yen Press, LLC.
The Yen On name and logo are trademarks of Yen Press, LLC.

The publisher is not responsible for websites (or their content) that are not owned by the publisher.

Library of Congress Cataloging-in-Publication Data
Names: Kagyū, Kumo, author. | Kannatuki, Noboru, illustrator.
Title: Goblin slayer / Kumo Kagyu ; illustration by Noboru Kannatuki.
Other titles: Goburin sureiyā. English
Description: New York, NY : Yen On, 2016–
Identifiers: LCCN 2016033529 | ISBN 9780316501590 (v. 1 : pbk.) | ISBN 9780316553223 (v. 2 : pbk.) | ISBN 9780316553230 (v. 3 : pbk.) | ISBN 9780316411882 (v. 4 : pbk.)
Subjects: LCSH: Goblins—Fiction. | GSAFD: Fantasy fiction.
Classification: LCC PL872.5.A367 G6313 2016 | DDC 895.63/6—dc23
LC record available at https://lccn.loc.gov/2016033529

ISBNs: 978-0-316-41188-2 (paperback)
978-0-316-44824-6 (ebook)

10 9 8 7 6

TPA

Printed in South Korea

GOBLIN SLAYER

Volume 4

GOBLIN SLAYER

A strange adventurer active on the frontier. He is famous for reaching Silver (3rd) rank hunting only goblins.

PRIESTESS

Works with Goblin Slayer. A sweet young woman who must put up with her partner's antics.

HIGH ELF ARCHER

An elf girl who adventures with Goblin Slayer. A Ranger and a skilled archer.

COW GIRL

A girl who works on the farm where Goblin Slayer lives. The two are old friends.

GUILD GIRL

A girl who works at the Adventurers Guild. Goblin Slayer's preference for goblin slaying always helps her out.

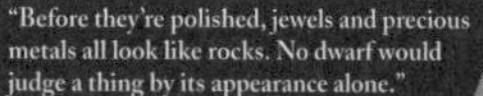

"Before they're polished, jewels and precious metals all look like rocks. No dwarf would judge a thing by its appearance alone."

DWARF SHAMAN

A dwarf spell caster who adventures with Goblin Slayer.

"A Naga does not run."

LIZARD PRIEST

A lizardman priest who adventures with Goblin Slayer.

"Train yourself: kill with the blade. If blood flows, let it be the enemy's."—First of the "Secrets of Steel."

HEAVY WARRIOR

A Silver-ranked adventurer associated with the Guild in the frontier town. Along with Female Knight and his other companions, his party is one of the best on the frontier.

"Only a tangled skein awaits those who carelessly spin tales about love or the universe's mysteries...not to mention a woman's beauty."

WITCH

A Silver-ranked adventurer at the frontier town's Adventurers Guild.

"I won't make friends tomorrow with an enemy I respect. I'll do it today."

SPEARMAN

A Silver-ranked adventurer at the frontier town's Adventurers Guild.

"Love does not consist in gazing at each other, but in looking outward in the same direction."—A poet

SWORD MAIDEN

Archbishop of the Temple of the Supreme God in the water town. Also a Gold-ranked adventurer who once fought with the Demon Lord.

A shining star: the promise of a hundred suns in the heavens.

A colored thread: one stitch in a finished cloth.

A drop of rain: one fleck of a surging sea.

An adventurer's scar: one story in a hero's legend.

A thousand thousands; ten thousand ten thousands: together they rise higher than the mountains.

Thus the world is made, regardless of how the dice may fall.

CHAPTER 1

Of Rookie Warrior and Apprentice Priestess

The cheap blade cut through the miasma with a *fwwsh*, and a giant rat, fat and round, came flying at them.

"Eeyikes!"

Its wide, dirty front teeth were sharp, its malodorous breath summoning images of their untimely demise.

Overwhelmed, he stumbled backward, batting at the creature with his well-used round shield.

"GYURI?!"

The rat fell to the ground with a cry, but it quickly scrambled up again. No damage.

Rookie Warrior shook out his left arm, which had gone numb from the impact despite the shield, and tried to regain his footing.

"Come on, why didn't you hit it back?"

"My whole arm hurts!"

Behind him, Apprentice Priestess admonished him in her strident, nasal voice. She held a combined sword-and-scales in one hand and a lantern in the other while frowning deeply.

The sewers reeked with a rotten stench that threatened to turn his stomach. Even keeping his nose blocked didn't help.

The slick footing. Wastewater flowing nearby. Giant rats with a bite that threatened much worse than simple pain. The vermin that writhed everywhere.

All of this was no different from normal. But it still put Rookie Warrior on the verge of tears.

One day down here, one gold coin in your pocket, they say.

That was if you met your quota. And that was an important source of income for making a living.

Still, shouldn't adventurers at least be dealing with goblins or something…?

"Watch out, dummy, here it comes!"

"—?!"

His friend's shout brought his attention back, and he heaved a great thrust with his sword, not even looking where he aimed.

"GYAARU?!?!"

He pierced fur and flesh and sinewy heart. The sensation was unpleasant.

It was accompanied by a gush of warm liquid that spattered across the boy's face.

He leaned against the thrashing hunk of meat and cried out.

"H-hrkk…?!"

When he shoved the rat off his sword, it fell, still twitching, to the ground.

The black pool of blood at his feet seeped across the ground, soaking his boots.

"Hey, are you all right? It didn't bite you?"

"Y-yeah, I'm fine."

"………..Okay."

Apprentice Priestess put on her best show of nonchalance, but even so, she hurried to Rookie Warrior's side. Heedless of her white robes, she wiped at the blood on his cheek, and some smeared her fingers.

"It didn't get in your eyes, did it? What about your mouth?"

"Ugh. A little."

"What were you doing? Gosh."

With an exasperated mutter, she took an antidote out of the bag of items she was carrying.

Rookie Warrior was spitting out blood and washing his mouth with the canteen. He downed the bitter antidote gratefully.

Both of them were still Porcelain rank. For them, the Cure miracle, for healing poison, was as much a dream as full plate armor or a suit of mail.

Still, they could not be underestimated—as the former monster, now an inert lump on the floor, could attest.

The rat had been busy with something: a corpse clad in rags. The figure's empty eye sockets and ruined cheekbones suggested a vagrant, but around its gnawed-out throat hung a level tag.

Apprentice Priestess took the porcelain-colored tag, wrapped it gently in a handkerchief, and put it in her bag.

The unfortunate girl—they knew she was a girl, for the tag identified her as such—had not been wearing any armor. She had gone down into the sewers with nothing but her clothes and a stick, and the rats, most likely, had eaten her.

"...Ugh," Rookie Warrior said. "They're back."

"Don't sound so unhappy. This is our job, isn't it?"

Perhaps it was the death of its kin that drew it, or simply the smell of spilt blood, but another rat had appeared from the sewer depths.

The creature was bigger than an infant child, its shadow wavering in the lantern light.

"We need the ear to prove we killed it," said Apprentice Priestess. "Quick, cut it off before it gets chewed on!"

"The ear? Me?"

"Just do it!"

"You could act just a little more concerned for me, you know..."

Even as he muttered, the boy grabbed the hilt of his sword, still stuck in the rat's carcass, and gave it a tug.

"...Huh?"

It wouldn't come out.

No matter how hard he pulled, the sword, lodged firmly in the meat, refused to budge.

He braced himself for leverage against the corpse—now weirdly soft after its violent passing—but to no avail.

And as he stood there struggling, one of the live rats, its eyes burning brightly, was drawing ever nearer.

"N-no—!" he gasped. "H-hold on a minute...!"

"Here it comes! Do something, dummy, it's getting closer!"

"E-eeyikes!"

It was the work of an instant:

Rookie Warrior tumbled backward to avoid the rat's jaws, landing in a pile of waste. The rotten food, or whatever it was, slopped over him, but it was better than being bitten and risking an infection. A critical hit from those teeth and his throat could be torn out altogether.

"GURUUURRRU...!"

The giant rat growled, whipping its tail back and forth, menacing Rookie Warrior. It probably saw the unarmed boy and the little girl studiously hanging back behind him as simply more food. It looked at them as a bit of saliva dribbled from its mouth, the very image of hunger. It obviously had no intention of letting them get away.

Of course, if they ran, the adventurers would not get to eat, either—albeit for more indirect reasons.

"Ahhh, darn it all!" Apprentice Priestess gave an unmannerly click of her tongue.

Giant rats...Giant rats spread illness and are dirty and one is attacking us right now, and they are enemies of Order—enemies of Order!

She seemed to be trying to remind herself of all this as she lifted the sword-and-scales high and as light began to build around it. It grew into a sword of lightning.

"Lord of judgment, sword-prince, scale-bearer, display here your power!"

And then Holy Smite, which she had called forth from the gods, pierced the rat with its blade.

Emitting a wisp of smoke and the smell of burning flesh, the giant rat soared through the air before bouncing and rolling over, dead.

The boy pursed his lips with a sound of displeasure as the girl let out a relieved breath.

"Lucky you. The gods make everything nice and easy, don't they?"

"Oh, save it. You know I can only call on them once per day." Apprentice Priestess glared at Rookie Warrior for his show of disrespect. "Anyway, hurry up and get your sword. I want to collect those ears and then go home and take a long bath."

"Yeah, sure."

Rookie Warrior approached the body of the first rat hesitantly, and this time put his whole strength into extracting his sword.

Then…

Scrrrape.

"…"

"…"

It was a sound they did not like. The two adventurers looked at each other at the unexpected noise, stiff with fright.

Scrr…

Scrape.

Scrrrape…

Scrape.

The sound came from deep in the darkness.

Trembling, Apprentice Priestess raised the lantern.

Something black and glimmering resolved into the shape of a huge insect. It shone as though covered in oil. One of them, two…then many, many more. Even at a quick count, it was clear they numbered greater than ten.

While reaching out with their long, thin antennae, the creatures approached slowly.

They were coming straight for the adventurers, jaws wide.

"Oh—"

Apprentice Priestess's voice caught in her throat, before—

"Noooooooo!"

"Idiot! Don't shout, run!"

The pair grabbed what they could and scrambled out of the sewers in a panic.

A terrible scraping sound told them the black insects were still right on their heels.

How far was it to the exit, again?

Rookie Warrior reflected: he wouldn't ask for a dragon. Maybe goblins, at least—although they could drag out your final moments and make it horrific. But of all things, the way he least wanted to die was to be eaten alive by giant roaches.

§

The spring twilight was warm, as if heralding the coming of summer.

"Hrg…ggrrh…"

Rookie Warrior woke to a morning light that pierced his eyes, stretching on the hay to work out his stiff body.

He took a deep breath and exhaled, the air an unpleasant blend of alcohol and animal musk.

Greeting a new day in the stables was still better than being in the sewers.

The Adventurers Guild had an inn, of course, but it wasn't free. True, they were all "economy" rooms—though the beds were just blankets pulled over wooden boards.

They were hardly suites, but…

"I just don't have the money."

He let out a slow breath. The previous day's adventure went firmly in the "loss" column of his finances.

One antidote, one sword, and—because they hadn't met the requested quota—no reward.

He could survive today, because he at least had some money he had scrimped and saved in the past. But at this rate, it wouldn't be long before he would have to cart his meager possessions back home, or—if he was especially unlucky—maybe even become a serf or a prostitute.

It had only been a few months earlier that Rookie Warrior had rushed away from his small farming village to become an adventurer. The reason was that Apprentice Priestess, an old friend of his, had set out to train and seemed likely to die if left to her own devices.

Her perspective, on the other hand, was that *she* had accompanied *him* on "some kind of warrior training or something" so he didn't get left for dead in the underbrush somewhere.

He felt he would have to set her straight on this matter at some point.

Well, *had* felt.

In the months since they had come to the frontier town, they had done nothing but kill rats. And sometimes roaches.

Is this really adventuring work…?

It was enough to cause his dreams to wither on the vine, breaking down his certainty and resolve.

"Stop it, stop it. That's enough with that kind of thinking."

He gave himself a shake and plucked a stray piece of hay out of his clothes.

Nearby, a middle-aged man, apparently also an adventurer, snoozed in the deep sleep of a drunk, snoring noisily.

Across from them, the horses shot dirty looks at the humans who presumed to share their sleeping space.

He didn't see Apprentice Priestess anywhere.

As disappointed as he had been, Rookie Warrior still had enough pride to allow her to sleep in one of those simple beds.

"Hokay! Today's another day!"

Pretending to be in a good mood is close enough to actually being in a good mood, right? He gave a yell, grabbed his stuff, and raced out of the stable.

Heading straight to the well, he drew up a bucket and splashed water all over his face. Using the cloth at his waist, he began scrubbing vigorously. There were still no signs of any new ability to grow a beard.

"I'll start to look more like a hero soon…I hope."

Or maybe facial hair would just give Apprentice Priestess a reason to point and laugh at him. Rookie Warrior groaned.

In any case, there was a lot to do.

With the minor task of making himself presentable out of the way, the boy went straight back to the stables. He grabbed a small spade from the rack of farm tools and headed around back.

"Hmmm. Now, where did I put it…?"

The exhausted state he had been in upon returning the night before left him with only a hazy recollection of what was where.

He rustled about on the ground for a minute, searching for something, before, with an "Ah, it's there," he found the most recent traces of disturbed earth.

He drove the shovel into the dirt, bracing a foot against it and digging for a while.

After a bit of work, he pulled his equipment out of the ground—his armor and shield.

He had had them made shortly after arriving in town, using his meager funds. They were cheap, but without equal. This was equipment he knew he could rely on.

There was, of course, a reason he had buried them.

"...Erk. They stink...hrrm. Well, still for the best, I guess."

He brought his face close to them and sniffed.

Tumbling into the pile of sewage hadn't bothered him when they had been in a hurry to escape. The problem had been when they got back to the surface, and he had realized just how bad it smelled. Not only people in the street, but even his fellow adventurers wrinkled their noses and frowned at him.

In the end, when they had returned to the Guild to make their report, the receptionist had smilingly said, "Please go clean up, then come back."

All the while Apprentice Priestess had stood there, bright red and shaking, staring at the ground...

We messed up..., he had thought slowly.

In the end, although he wasn't much used to it, he washed his clothes, dried them, and rinsed himself off before changing.

After some consideration about what to do with his leather armor and shield, he had decided the only thing was to bury them in the ground and hope it would take some of the stench off.

The odor had improved a little, or so he hoped, so he wiped off the dirt with a cloth and equipped himself.

He wouldn't have had the courage to leave his precious equipment simply lying around even if he had been in a rented room, much less staying in the stables as he was.

"Erk..."

His stomach began rumbling, accompanied by a painful sensation.

Rookie Warrior instinctively put a hand to his abdomen and looked around with a touch of panic. There was no one there. No one around to hear.

Now that he thought about it, he had only had some water to drink the day before.

The sky was blue, the morning sun shining brightly.

Rookie Warrior heaved a sigh.

"...Guess I better get something to eat."

§

"...You're late."

Apprentice Priestess was already at the tavern.

She was in the corner, and the room was alive with adventurers even at this early hour.

She was resting her chin on her hands and looking annoyed; Rookie Warrior sat at the table with a short apology.

"Oh," he added, "and good morning. Breakfast?"

"I already ate," Apprentice Priestess said brusquely, but then she muttered her response to his greeting. "Morning. Anyway. Just hurry up and eat. I want to head down again in the afternoon if we can."

There was an empty bread plate in front of her. At his seat, there were beans, bacon soup, and bread.

Rookie Warrior opened his mouth in confusion, closed it, then opened it again.

"I'm sorry."

"For what?"

"Ahh..."

It seemed like if he said anything else, he would just make her angry again.

And there's no need to fight first thing in the morning.

He took a spoon and brought some soup to his mouth. Apprentice Priestess gave a *hmph.*

"And your clothes. Are they still hanging behind the stable?"

"Oh, uh, yeah." Rookie Warrior nodded. He took a bite of hard bread and swallowed. "They weren't dry yet."

"Okay, give them to me later. That stink will never come out the way you wash them. I'll do it for you."

"Oh, uh...sorry."

"I don't want to end up stinky just because I hang out with you." And then she turned away from him.

The failure of their last outing had been entirely his fault. "Sorry," he murmured, focusing on his food.

He tore off a piece of bread, dipping it in the soup. When it was good and soggy, he scooped up some bacon with his spoon and ate everything together. The soup was thin and tasted mostly of salt. He ate without a word, dutifully.

If the guy who was supposed to be the shield was so hungry he couldn't move, what would their small party do then? This was another part of his job.

All finished, he tossed his spoon on top of his empty plate and nodded.

"Okay. Weapons."

"It's a waste just to leave that sword down there."

"No, but listen," he said back, pouring some water from the carafe on the table into his glass. "I need a weapon if we're going to go back and find it."

"And do you have the money?"

"About that…"

He gulped down his water. Apprentice Priestess reached for the carafe at the same moment he did, so he filled her glass.

"Thanks," she said, putting both hands around her glass and bringing it to her lips. "You don't have any, do you? Money, I mean."

"Maybe I could borrow…"

"Stop that. Don't take on any debt."

"Nah. I mean loaner gear or something."

Borrow a weapon. He thought about some of his acquaintances, wondering if any of them would be willing to lend something.

It might be easy enough to get his hands on a dagger, but that didn't inspire much confidence.

And to borrow anything like a longsword—like the one he'd lost with a single swing—would count against him.

Trust was not such an easy thing to come by.

He was just giving a deep, involuntary sigh when…

"Hm? What's up, kid? Pretty early in the morning for such a long face."

The lighthearted comment sounded above him.

His head jerked up. He saw an adventurer carrying a spear that glinted in the light.

The tag that hung around his neck was Silver—the third rank.

"Oh, uh, well…"

"I've got a date, by which I mean an adventure, so I don't have long. But I'll listen while I can."

Rookie Warrior suddenly found himself lost for words. Spearman, renowned as "the frontier's strongest," beamed a friendly smile toward him.

The young warrior swallowed. Next to him, Apprentice Priestess jabbed an elbow into his side. He nodded resolutely.

"Uh, actually, I…I lost my weapon on our adventure yesterday."

"Oh yeah?" Spearman frowned instinctively. "That's rough," he said, his voice tinged with apparent sincerity.

"I want to go get it back, but I don't have a weapon, so…I was thinking maybe there was a chance someone would loan me one…"

"A spare you can borrow, huh? …I've got some extras, so I could let you use one, but…" Spearman looked Rookie Warrior over from head to toe, then concluded: "I'm not sure you have the strength for it."

"Erk…"

The slightest sound of embarrassment escaped him.

Rookie Warrior was thin and flexible, but in terms of muscles, he was no match for Spearman.

They just had different body types. Naturally they would use weapons of differing weights.

"And if you lost this one, too, I'll bet you couldn't pay me back."

"True, yes?" *Even he can't bring himself to extort money from a junior adventurer.*

A beautiful woman appeared at Spearman's side, quiet as a shadow except for her murmured words.

She was a witch who wore clothes that accentuated her full, voluptuous figure. Apprentice Priestess found her face turning red, and she averted her eyes.

"And a magical weapon, would surely not, suit you well, no?"

A loaner magical weapon?!

Rookie Warrior's eyes bulged as Witch whispered and giggled.

For a beginner like him, metal armor was the stuff of dreams. A magical weapon might as well have been distant legend.

I hear you can find them in ruins and labyrinths if you're really lucky, and I do see them for sale occasionally.

But they were several digits too expensive for him to ever think of owning one.

"So instead, let me, give you something, good."

Witch retrieved something from her neckline with an elegant motion—a single candle.

It didn't appear to be the usual white, but bluish—which was, on close inspection, because of the colored letters covering it.

The profusion of characters was carved into the candle in a flowing script that Rookie Warrior could not decipher.

"It's..." Apprentice Priestess blinked several times. "...a candle?"

"Yes."

Witch winked and lowered her voice as if she were revealing a deep, dark secret.

"This, see, is a seeking candle...When, you near, the object of your search, it gets, warmer. See?"

A magic item. Rookie Warrior swallowed hard.

There was no need for them to use it themselves. If they sold it, it would bring in more than enough for a good sword...

"Feel free, to, sell it—turn, it into money."

Her smile seemed to see right through him, and Rookie Warrior found himself staring at the ground. Apprentice Priestess gave him another poke in the side with her elbow.

"Oh, um. I, uh— Th-thanks. Thank you very much."

"Not, at all. A little, something, to help."

Rookie Warrior received the item hesitantly as Witch wore an amused expression and smiled.

"Well, then. We have our...date."

"Yep. Don't die, kids."

Spearman gave Rookie Warrior's hair a parting ruffle and set off at a jaunty pace.

Witch followed right behind him through the Guild doors.

Rookie Warrior set his right hand on his head, where he could still feel that powerful palm.

"...They're so cool."

"Yeah." Apprentice Priestess allowed herself a whisper. "Perhaps..."

§

"Uh-uh, nope, no way!" In the grassy field behind the Guild, Scout Boy was seated and waving his hands frantically. "I lost my own dagger recently. The one I have now is borrowed. If I lent it out, Cap would kill me!"

"You lost it? What happened?"

"It got dissolved by a giant slug."

"What are you doing?" the rhea Druid Girl asked, raising her eyebrows.

"A giant slug, huh? Lucky you…"

Rookie Warrior pursed his lips, receiving an elbow in the side from Apprentice Priestess. "We're Porcelain-ranked, while they're in a Silver party. We can't compare."

"You were killing giant rats, right?" Scout Boy asked. Rookie Warrior frowned and nodded.

"And I lost my sword doing it."

"You're just lucky it wasn't a one-of-a-kind item."

Scout Boy glanced up at where Heavy Warrior was swinging his massive two-handed blade.

There was a *whoosh* as it sliced through the air, and then a *thud* as Female Knight leaped in.

The two-handed sword prevented him from carrying a shield, but the ease with which he wielded it was a testament to the magic power he'd been given.

Strike, block, hit, parry, slam, overhead swing, deflect, cut, repel.

His weapon was finely crafted, as was his armor. The shine of the carefully worked weapon was unmistakable even in the sunlight.

"…Wish I had one of those."

"One of what?"

"That greatsword," Rookie Warrior said, resting his chin on his hands. "A two-handed blade."

"Forget it," Apprentice Priestess said, her eyes widening. "Even if you had one, think what would happen."

"Yeah, whatever."

"Does she mean he'd only ever cut thin air?"

"She means he'd never hit anything."

Scout Boy and Druid Girl's chatter caused Rookie Warrior to turn away in annoyance.

"If I did hit something, though, it'd be awesome."

"Those weapons are so heavy, you'd be exhausted before long."

"But I'd look really cool."

"And they're not cheap, either." Apprentice Priestess wagged her finger reprovingly at Rookie Warrior, and there was nothing he could do but keep quiet.

"It's like she cast Silence on you!" Scout Boy barked a laugh. "Boy, has she got you under her thumb!"

"Oh," Druid Girl said with a quiet snort and a calm expression, flicking her leaf-shaped ears. "As though you wouldn't waste all our money if I didn't hold the purse strings."

Scout Boy had brought the rebuke on himself. He gave a click of his tongue, and Druid Girl nodded in satisfaction. Then she asked, "Hey, what if you asked the Guild for advice?"

"You mean about borrowing a weapon?"

"No, how to kill giant rats. Maybe they have some tips."

"Hmmm." Apprentice Priestess made a low sound. "I wonder if it could be that easy."

§

"I'm afraid it's not that easy."

Of course not.

Guild Girl shook her head slowly at Apprentice Priestess, putting her hand to her cheek and looking troubled.

"I thought not..."

"We ask adventurers to do it because it's not easy, essentially."

"If anyone could do it, there wouldn't be any work, huh...," Rookie Warrior said. "Oh, one antidote, please."

"Of course, here you go."

Apprentice Priestess took the proffered bottle and stowed it carefully in her item bag. At least the bitter memory of when she had run and tripped, shattering one inside her pack, served a purpose.

"Say, how about a healing potion?" added Guild Girl.

"I'd love one, but…you know, the money… Do you have any bandages, or herbs, or ointments?"

"It really isn't that easy, is it? Still, though…" Guild Girl cleared her throat with an air of importance. "There may be something I can teach you…"

"Really?!" Rookie Warrior rattled his chair as he leaned out over the counter.

It was past noon, and there were few other adventurers to be seen in the Adventurers Guild.

Most of them had already selected their quests and set off enthusiastically for adventure.

Rookie Warrior and Apprentice Priestess had waited until this moment to ask for help, and they would have hated to go home without so much as a single hint.

"Anything! Anything at all!"

"Well, it really is a very obvious idea…" Guild Girl raised her pointer finger, which emphasized the neatly trimmed nail. "Strengthen your defense. At least have some chain mail, or something similar, so the rats and giant roaches can't bite you."

"But we don't have any money…!" All of Rookie Warrior's excitement dissipated, and the chair clattered again as he slumped back, his voice utterly dejected.

Guild Girl leaned her head to the side, causing her roughly braided hair to spill down.

"You can get a slight discount if you buy used equipment."

"Don't they get that from dead people?" Apprentice Priestess asked a bit coldly, and Guild Girl made a *how rude* sound of displeasure.

"Some of it comes from retired adventurers, or people who traded up. We don't carry anything cursed."

"But you do have items from dead people, right?"

"Well, we… But never if they became undead…" Guild Girl looked hesitant for a moment. But soon she wore her smile again. "Anyway, gear is gear, right?"

Rookie Warrior heaved a sigh.

And no money is no money.

"Any other ideas…?"

"Let's see... Oh, are you using a lantern?"

"Yes, the one from the Adventurer's Toolkit," Apprentice Priestess said a bit wearily. The Adventurer's Toolkit contained rope, a lantern, chalk, and several lengths of chain, all in one place. So far, only the lantern had been much use to them, and she sort of regretted buying it.

"There are people who use a torch instead of a lantern, because it doubles as a weapon."

Guild Girl mentioned with a smile that rats and insects both despised fire.

"What kind of adventurer would do something like that?"

"Well, for one—"

Guild Girl stopped suddenly, and it was as though a flower had bloomed across her face.

Rookie Warrior followed her gaze, finding the entrance to the Guild.

The saloon-style doors creaked open, and the nose-prickling odor of iron came wafting in.

It was hard to blame Rookie Warrior for the "Ergh" that escaped him.

A most curious adventurer appeared in the entrance.

He wore a cheap-looking steel helmet and grimy leather armor, a small shield was tied to his arm, and a primitive club hung at his waist.

He was the adventurer called Goblin Slayer.

"G-Goblin Slayer, sir, I told you, it's too soon..."

"Is it?"

A priestess in white vestments soiled to a gruesome red-black came hurrying in after him.

Goblin Slayer's reply was brief. He acknowledged the two at the reception counter, then started walking with his bold stride. He sat down on the bench in the waiting area with a thump. Priestess collapsed next to him.

Guild Girl, wiggling her fingers down by her side in a sort of signal, squinted as if to say, *It can't be helped.*

"You have to clean up. I'm always telling you. People will misunderstand," she grumbled. Then she noticed the expressions on the faces of Rookie Warrior and Apprentice Priestess. "Are you two all right?"

"Oh, we, uh…"

"Um…" Apprentice Priestess scratched her cheek awkwardly. "We said something rather…rude, before."

She was talking about something from several months earlier, but the event was still fresh in their memories.

They had thought he might be trying to use his rookie companion as bait.

Now it seemed like a terribly inappropriate thing to think, but at the time they had been convinced they had to rescue Priestess.

"Ah!" said Guild Girl with a giggle, catching on. "I'm sure it's fine. He doesn't let those sorts of things bother him."

"Yeah, but it bothers us…" Rookie Warrior said, and then blinked. He rubbed his eyes with his sleeve. Something was off.

The newcomer wore a cheap-looking steel helmet and grimy leather armor, a small shield was tied to his arm, and a primitive club was at his waist.

A club?

"…Doesn't he use a sword?"

"Now that you mention it…" Apprentice Priestess looked in Goblin Slayer's direction, too. "…I guess he does. A really cheap-looking one, though."

"Yeah, you're right."

"And that girl is covered in blood spatters…"

What in the world happened? The young pair looked very worried, but Guild Girl only gave a chuckle and a smile.

"Wondering about them?" she asked, pointedly tapping some papers against her desk to straighten them. "The best way to learn about adventuring is to ask an adventurer."

"S-sure…"

But that person was Goblin Slayer.

Then again, he was also an adventurer of the third, Silver, rank.

But…he was also Goblin Slayer…

"…Okay, then!"

It was Apprentice Priestess who stood up with all the enthusiasm she could muster.

"H-hey, what—?"

"Asking," she said, staring fixedly forward, "costs nothing!"

Then she left the floundering Rookie Warrior and started marching forward with an air of determination.

Rookie Warrior glanced at Guild Girl. She was still smiling.

"Aww, man…!"

Now Rookie Warrior rallied himself and stood.

Guild Girl's expression, of course, never changed.

§

"Umm…," Apprentice Priestess called out, eliciting only a tired "Wuh?" from Priestess.

It was clear she had just finished an adventure with Goblin Slayer. Apprentice Priestess frowned, only now realizing that she should have chosen a better time.

"What is it?"

"Eep…"

And on top of that, there was that low-pitched, dispassionate, almost mechanical voice.

The steel helmet moved slowly, with a piercing gaze beyond the visor. The man's armor was covered in dark bloodstains.

He really does look like living armor or something…

With that rather untoward thought in her head, Apprentice Priestess swallowed.

"Uh— Um!" Rookie Warrior broke in as if to cover for her. He ignored her complaint of *Just a second!* and continued in a familiar tone.

"There's something we'd like to ask you…if it's okay."

"What is it?"

Goblin Slayer's reply was brief, and it was delivered in that same low-pitched voice.

Next to him, Priestess's head was bobbing from side to side.

"Quietly, please."

"Oh—erk… S-sorry…" Rookie Warrior replied in a strained voice. His hands were stiff, and shaking a bit from nervousness.

Apprentice Priestess took his hand gently. It was rough and covered in scars.

"…Was it pretty bad, this job?"

"We needed some money." *But, no.* Goblin Slayer shook the helmet from side to side. "I was made to go along."

Rookie Warrior swallowed heavily and squeezed Apprentice Priestess's hand back.

"Well, we… We wanted to ask you something." He took a single deep breath. His hands relaxed. "Why are you using a club?"

The answer came in a single swoop: "I stole it from a goblin."

"S-stole it?"

"You throw a blade, or stab with it. It breaks or chips. Careful use can help, but a single sword is not good for more than five of them."

That sort of sounded like an answer… And then again, sort of not.

Wait… Maybe it is.

"Hrrm," grunted Rookie Warrior. Then he paused for a long moment. "What about rats or roaches?"

Now it was Goblin Slayer's turn to grunt. "Rats or roaches?"

"…Yeah."

"I couldn't tell you." *But…* He tapped the club at his belt. "…If you swing this and hit with it, you will damage them. At least you don't have to worry about the blade chipping."

Goblin Slayer rose from the bench, tremendously slowly. Priestess, who had been leaning on him, gave a shudder.

"It's easy."

"Easy…"

"I'm going," he said briefly to Rookie Warrior, who stood thinking. Then the helmet turned to where Priestess was wiping the sleep from her eyes. "Resting?"

"Oh, n-no, I'm coming!"

"I see."

Priestess stood, too, hurrying to keep up with the bold pace that carried him quickly away.

But just on the verge of setting off, she turned to the other two adventurers and gave a small bow.

"Oh, um—hey!" Apprentice Priestess said.

"Yes?"

It was now or never.

Apprentice Priestess had called out almost without thinking, but now Priestess tilted her head. "Can I help you?"

"Well, um, we just... Why are you covered in blood?"

"Oh..." Priestess murmured with a look of mild confusion. She blushed ever so slightly. "I...I'd just as soon you...not ask."

"Oh...oh really?"

"Ah, b-but, I'm not hurt or anything, so don't worry!" She gave Apprentice Priestess a tired but gallant smile. She was covered in sweat and dirt, but there was no hint of a shadow to her expression.

The level tag that hung at her neck was not Porcelain, but Obsidian.

Apprentice Priestess let out a breath.

"Hey..."

"Yes?"

"Sorry about before."

"?"

"I think we *seriously* misunderstood what was going on."

Priestess's eyes widened, and she blinked several times. "—Don't worry about it!" And then suddenly, the calm, serious girl gripped her staff with both hands. "It's totally fine. I know how he looks, but he's a good person..."

"Not coming?" a gruff voice called from a ways off.

"We should talk when we get a chance," Priestess said, and then she bowed to the two of them. Putting one hand on her head to keep her cap on, she ran over to where Goblin Slayer stood.

"Anything wrong?" he asked.

But she replied, "No, nothing."

"You're exhausted?"

"Oh, no... Um. Well, maybe I'm a little tired."

"Rest a bit."

Even from a distance, the two of them could see Priestess smile just a little as she answered, "Yes, sir."

Apprentice Priestess exhaled and shrugged her shoulders.

"I guess…"

"Huh?"

"We'll have to try our best, too."

"Uh-huh!"

With that, Rookie Warrior and Apprentice Priestess gently bumped their fists together.

§

"All riiiight! Here we go!"

"Okay, let's go down the list!"

On the outskirts of town, just after dawn, with the bluish-purple haze of morning still hanging in the air, the voices of a boy and girl could be heard near the sewage ditch.

"Antidote!"

"Check!"

"First-aid supplies!"

"Ointments and herbs, check!"

"Light!"

"The lantern from the Adventurer's Toolkit, some oil, and a torch! What about you?"

"The Seeking Candle… Umm, map!"

"Check! By which I mean I borrowed it when we accepted our quest."

"Fair enough. Now, armor!"

"My leather armor still kind of stinks…my shield, too. Here, you give me a spin."

"Me? It's not like I plan to get attacked wearing these vestments."

"I don't care, just show me. Otherwise, what's the point of a checklist?"

"Yeah, fine… Last, weapons!"

"Check!"

And with that, Rookie Warrior took his primitive, but brand-new, club in his right hand.

It was so pristine, it might still have had a price tag attached. The average buyer would have considered it a cheap item, but the young man could hardly think it so.

"Good," Apprentice Priestess said, nodding at the club. She spread her arms wide and spun around once. The sleeves of her white garment puffed out. There were seams and tears in places, but it was still clean and attractive.

"Look okay?"

"You might want to do some mending later."

"If I have anything to mend with..." Apprentice Priestess put her hands on her hips and, with a serious expression, gave a shout. "If we don't meet our quota today, that's it! We're finished!"

"I don't think things are quite that bad..."

"But that's the attitude you have to go in with!"

Rookie Warrior seemed to be relaxed; Apprentice Priestess gave him a smart smack with her sword-and-scales. "We don't even have the money to go back home. You would end up a serf, and I would be...you know..."

"A prostitute? Pfft, who would take you?"

"How dare you say that, jerk!" Her face turned bright red, and her elbow found the boy's side—right where his armor was tied.

She looked at him quivering and writhing, and then she snorted.

"Anyway, you understand?"

"Y-yeah, I do, but... Well, yeah." Rookie Warrior steadied himself, adjusted his grip on his items, and nodded energetically. "We'll manage it somehow!"

This was a frontier town, one of the places people had labored to claim, and there was a sewer here because, of course, someone had built it.

It was one thing when a city was built above some old ruins, like the water town was, but there were no public services in an unoccupied field. Dwarven craftsmen and wizards, accomplished builders of all sorts, had been called in to create the stone sewer from scratch.

Had the sewer been built because the town was prospering, or had the town prospered because the sewer was built? Rookie Warrior did not know which had come first.

Heck, I don't even know how it works.

Beyond the rusted metal doors and down a flight of stairs was a dim, dank stone dungeon.

A walkway ran along the canal that carried the wastewater, and a rotten stench drifted across everything.

Without hesitating, Rookie Warrior covered his mouth with a cloth; Apprentice Priestess scrunched up her face and put in nose plugs.

The sewer was new, but giant rats and giant roaches were drawn to filth.

For some reason, Non-Praying Characters—the NPCs—seemed to naturally appear in such places. All the more reason to get rid of them before some even bigger threat came along…

"So which way do we go?"

"Oh, um, hang on!"

As Rookie Warrior stood with what, for him, passed for constant vigilance, Apprentice Priestess hurriedly fished something out.

She took a flint and lit the lantern, then hung it at her waist. She opened it and touched the flame to the candle.

The Seeking Candle burned with a weird blue-white flame; she could feel it getting gradually warmer in her hand.

"…How is it?"

"It's warm, but still just kind of…"

"Be sure to keep my sword firmly in your mind."

They were there to find a sword, true, but they were also there to kill rats. They had a quota to meet.

Rookie Warrior, determined that they would accomplish everything they had come for, set off, turning down several sewer tunnels until finally they found themselves deep within.

It was the nest of the giant rats, which they had finally located after their many dives in search of it.

"…Ooh, here they are."

Perhaps it was the current that brought so much of the food waste from town here.

That was what the oversized rats were after. One of them, two…

Rookie Warrior spat on his hand and rubbed it into the hilt of his weapon, then he dove at the creatures.

"Yaaaaaahh!"

"GYUUI?!"

One of them fled from him, but he took the one that was focused on its meal.

There was a blunt sound of impact that was entirely different from striking with a sword. He felt the weapon connect with the lump of flesh.

The giant rat screeched and tumbled away, but it was still alive.

"You—die—now!"

He had long ago discarded any sense of sympathy for the monsters. It was kill or be killed. If they got their teeth in his windpipe, it was he who would die.

"Whoa! Yah!"

The giant rat jumped up and leaped at him, fangs bared.

Rookie Warrior met it with his shield, throwing his weight behind it in a body blow. His left arm, the one with the shield on it, tingled with the impact of a hunk of meat weighing nearly ten kilograms.

"Why—you—!"

But Rookie Warrior had the advantage when it came to body weight.

He braced himself against the grimy walkway to keep from tumbling, then brought his club down on the rat's head.

There was no technique, no secret. A back-alley fistfight had more sophistication.

"GYU?!"

There was a crack like the breaking of a wet branch as the rat's spine broke. Another blow. The giant rat twitched.

He checked that its eyes were empty, and only then did Rookie Warrior finally wipe the sweat from his brow.

"Wh-what about the o-other one…?!"

"It already ran away."

Rookie Warrior scanned the area, while the girl nervously holding the sword-and-scales let out a breath.

She walked briskly up to him and with a practiced eye checked him over for any wounds.

Rookie Warrior closed his hand as if making sure it still worked, then opened it; then he shifted his arms and legs as well.

He was unhurt. He hadn't been bitten. The rat was frothing blood, but none of it had gotten on him.

"I'm…fine."

"…Looks like it."

Good. Apprentice Priestess nodded. They wouldn't need to use their antidote or any of their healing items.

"So how did the club work out?"

"I'm not real sure yet…" Rookie Warrior gave a careless swing of the weapon. It wasn't sharp like a sword, but it was heavier than one, and that made it feel oddly trustworthy. "But I do know that if I hit something with it, it dies."

He couldn't help a sigh, thinking how far he was from the breezy attitude of Spearman or the sturdiness of Heavy Warrior.

It was just one rat.

But it was a good start.

§

"What's the candle say?"

"Hm…I guess this way is a little warmer?"

Each time they came to a fork in the road, Apprentice Priestess would hold up the candle to find the right direction, and then they would proceed.

Unfortunately—if perhaps predictably—the sword was not where they had left it after the previous day's battle. Maybe the giant rats had carried it off, or the giant roaches had pushed it aside…

"They're not goblins. They aren't just hoarding loot."

"Hey, don't say that, it's scary." Apprentice Priestess glared at Rookie Warrior and gave him another jab with her elbow. "If they were really goblins living under this town, it wouldn't be funny."

"For sure."

Then they would have to ask Goblin Slayer for more than just advice.

They continued their diligent search, complaining about the stench.

Along the way, they met—and dispensed with—a total of three giant rats. And one giant roach.

The club was soon covered in a thick slime, already speaking to the story of its battles.

"I guess I didn't think about how it would make blood and…are those brains? …splatter."

"Well, you saw how dirty that goblin guy—" Apprentice Priestess stopped herself. "How dirty Goblin Slayer got."

The new weapon was heavy, too, and having to swing it over and over in battle tired him out much quicker than a sword.

"But I like how you can just swing it without having to aim."

"Just try not to lose it or anything."

"Yeah—"

Rookie Warrior grunted his agreement with this opinion as he peeked around a corner.

There only seemed to be regular-sized rats there at the moment, so there was no problem.

Beckoning to Apprentice Priestess behind him, he went ahead one step at a time.

Apprentice Priestess gave a little yelp at the rats' long tails as they stepped around the rodents.

"Oh, yeah…"

"What is it? Got another silly comment to make?"

"No." Rookie Warrior shook his head hurriedly, checked to the left and right to make sure they were safe, then sat in the path. "Do we have any string?"

"Will rope work?"

"Too thick."

"I've got some string for holding my hair back…"

"Thanks."

She dug through her bag, then handed the hair tie to him, saying, "Be sure to give it back." Then she crouched next to Rookie Warrior and watched intently as he set to some kind of work.

"When we get some money, I'll buy you a new one."

"It comes out of your share, okay?"

"Yeah, sure."

The job was fine, but simple enough. He wrapped the string firmly around the handle of the club until it made a loop of a specific size.

When he put his hand through it to hold the club…

"See? Now I won't drop it."

"Hmm…" Apprentice Priestess inspected the jury-rigged strap closely, then gave a snort. "That's a pretty good job, for you."

"Ouch, that hurts."

"When we get back, I'll put on a better one for you."

Apprentice Priestess stood with a giggle, but when she lifted the candle to check it—

"Whoa, yikes!"

—she nearly dropped it, frantically adjusting her grip to keep a hold on it.

"Hey, what's wrong?" Rookie Warrior stood, too, holding his club in case there was trouble.

He was inexperienced, but still looked around carefully, his shield up. The girl shook her head.

"It-it's nothing. Just…the candle's getting hotter and hotter."

"It's getting hotter? So that means…"

He could see that the bluish-white flame of the Seeking Candle had grown noticeably larger.

Rookie Warrior and Apprentice Priestess looked at each other.

"We must be getting close."

It was critically good luck that allowed him to sense that something was coming at them from above.

Rookie Warrior immediately moved to cover Apprentice Priestess, giving her a shove as he got them both out of the way.

"Eek! Wh-what are you—!"

"Idiot, look!"

It was like a massive black lump.

It must have been six feet long, almost twice the usual size. It had a lustrous carapace and six spined legs, and it was waving antennae that looked like lengths of thin steel wire and gnashing its sharp-toothed jaws.

"What's the candle say…?!"

"It's *really* hot!"

"Don't tell me it's *inside* that thing!"

The bug—it was beyond giant, a huge roach—scuttled toward them. The two screamed and started running.

§

"Wh-wh-what do we do?!"

"I wish I knew…!"

The massive black insect crawling indiscriminately across ceiling, floor, and walls was more than a little terrifying.

The pursuit itself wasn't the only scary thing. It was the thought of being eaten alive by that creature.

They hadn't become adventurers just to become a feast for some rats or roaches…!

"It'll catch us at this rate…!"

That they were still safe as they dashed desperately through the sewers was thanks to the speed of their reaction and the distance they'd had to begin with.

A giant roach was nowhere near as agile as a human—at least not a Porcelain-ranked adventurer.

But it was obvious they didn't have long before it caught and devoured them.

We have to get to the surface before… No, we'll never make it…!

They would have to climb a ladder to get aboveground. If they were attacked at that moment, it would be over. Regular roaches could fly. Giant ones probably could, too.

"How about we jump in the water?!"

"A lot of good that will do us if we catch the plague!"

"Okay then… A narrow tunnel! Maybe it won't be able to follow us!"

"It won't work! Roaches are extremely flexible!"

A narrow passageway might give them a moment's respite, but then the bug would squeeze itself in with them. Just the thought was enough to give him a chill. No tunnels, then.

"We have to fight!"

"But how?!"

The scratching made him viscerally sick, and it was coming closer.

Rookie Warrior looked down at the club in his hand.

If he hit the roach enough times, it would die. He was sure of that. But how to do it?

If I just swing at it, I'll never hit it.

It was so fast. If he couldn't stop it from moving, the battle would be hopeless. He just didn't have the skill.

"H-hey! Do you think you could hit it with Holy Smite?!"

"I don't know…! The gods are the ones who aim the spell, not me!"

"What if it were coming straight at you?!"

"In that case, maybe…!"

"Okay!"

Now he would have to think fast. If he was going to do it, he couldn't hesitate.

Rookie Warrior grabbed the lantern from Apprentice Priestess's waist.

"Yikes! H-hey, what are you—?!"

"You can scold me if we survive!"

Shouting even louder than Apprentice Priestess, Rookie Warrior looked back.

The humongous insect was right there, slime dribbling from its chomping jaws.

Rookie Warrior took a deep breath.

"Try this on for size!"

And then he threw the lantern right in front of the insect.

The impact with the floor shattered the lantern's cheap casing, and fire leaped up from the flame within.

The massive roach gave a screech, spread its wings, and rose into the air. The sight alone was enough to make them lose their will to fight it.

Rookie Warrior felt something warm and wet in his pants. He set his jaw to stop his chattering teeth.

"Now—do it!"

"—Ee—ehh—ahhh—!"

In response to Rookie Warrior's shout, Apprentice Priestess, who had been trembling dumbly, raised the sword-and-scales.

"Lord of judgment, sword-prince, scale-bearer, show here your power!"

A crackling bolt of lightning drove straight into the filthy bug.

There was a crack of thunder, and a brilliant, bluish-white light banished the dim darkness of the sewers. The miracle lasted only for an instant.

Smoke that reeked of ozone and burned chitin erupted from the monster, turning their stomachs.

The huge roach fell to the ground, its abdomen hideously exposed, struggling to rise again with its six limbs.

"H-hii—yaaaaaahhh!"

Rookie Warrior lifted his club and jumped at it. He scrambled onto the black abdomen, ignoring the thorny legs clawing at him, and shoved his shield against its jaws. Dark pincers dug into the oiled leather, but his focus was complete. With an animal scream, he raised the club and brought it down, striking, breaking, again and again.

He paid no heed to the slime flying from the jaws, nor to the blood seeping from his scratches. If he did, he would be killed.

The sweaty grip slipped from his hand. The string he had tied around it allowed him to regain his hold. And he struck again.

Strike and strike and strike and strike and strike and strike. *Whatever happens, just strike. As many blows as possible. Beat it until it dies.*

"Hoo…ahh…huff…ahh…"

Finally, he had reached his limit. He didn't have enough oxygen.

He tried to clear his head, his vision reddened by the heat of his body, but the effort made him dizzy. Then Apprentice Priestess was there, supporting him just as he thought he would fall over.

"Are—are you okay…?!"

"I…I think so."

The boy registered that he was covered from head to toe in the roach's juices. His right hand, gripping his club, was especially bad.

Where the insect's head should have been, there was only a spreading pool of fluids.

The six legs, scrabbling with the last vestiges of life, were still to be feared.

"Is it…still alive…?" Apprentice Priestess asked.

"K-keep back. It's…dangerous."

Rookie Warrior swallowed heavily, then drew his work dagger from his belt. He used it to saw through each leg at the lowest joint until it finally broke off. He had to do this, or they wouldn't be safe. Six times he did it, until his fingers were stiff and terribly painful. But it still wasn't over.

"Um…the abdomen, right?"

He held the dagger in a two-handed reverse grip, raised it, and then brought it down. There was a *fsssh* and a geyser of fluid from the body.

The blade hit something hard, and then Rookie Warrior steeled himself and reached into the roach's stomach. He pulled something out.

"Found it…"

He had no idea what the creature had been thinking when it ate this. But the sword he pulled out was unmistakably the one he had so eagerly bought, his first weapon.

"…Starting today, maybe I'll call this sword Chestburster, and this club Roach Slayer. What do you think?"

"I think you should stop talking stupid and drink this antidote, and then we should go home."

The boy cut a pathetic figure, every inch of him covered in slime. Some of the stuff had landed on the girl's waist, which had been bared when the lantern was torn away, and was steaming there.

The two of them pretended not to notice either of these things as they exchanged a dry smile at their great victory.

§

"Sigh…"

The sun was setting on the frontier town.

The two of them had washed head to toe in the river—studiously avoiding any glimpses of each other in only their underpants—and then gone to the Guild to make their report.

They had checked their equipment, restocked the supplies they had used, tended to their scratches, and finally paid for a simple place to sleep.

In the end, all that was left were several silver coins that Rookie Warrior now held in his hand.

This would be their savings. *But…how much were we even able to save?*

Squatting by the door to the Adventurers Guild, Rookie Warrior felt like sighing, too.

"Hey, what are you staring into space for, anyway?"

"Hmm…"

Apprentice Priestess, pressing a towel to her wet hair, was just next to him.

Rookie Warrior made a non-answer, his focus on the people coming and going through the door.

Adventurers of every stripe were heading out to town with their special items or coming into the Guild. Each and every one of them was loaded with equipment, fatigue mingling with a sense of achievement on their faces.

The boy and girl did not yet have enough experience to realize this meant no adventurers had died that day.

"I was just…thinking we've got a long way to go."

"Well, obviously," Apprentice Priestess said with a snort, sitting down next to Rookie Warrior. "A little progress each day! The trouble starts when you want more than that."

"W-well, sure, but…"

"Do your best, sacrifice, make your money, and live your life. Can't complain about that, can you?"

"W-well, sure, but…" The silver coins in his hand shimmered in the evening light. The bright glints from the metal hurt his eyes. "…We've got a long way to go."

"…That's true."

But I—even I—was able to deal with some giant rats and roaches today.

It wouldn't make for much of a legend, but there was no denying he had put his life on the line.

"All right! Let's get some decent food!" he said, and thrust the coins at Apprentice Priestess.

"…Yeah. I guess we can indulge a bit today."

Someday—someday—someday.

They wanted to be brave. They wanted to be heroes.

They wanted to be adventurers who might defeat a dragon.

The coins rattled in the girl's palm as she stood.

CHAPTER 2

Of a Certain Little Boy

"Come on, how late are you gonna sleep? Wake up!"

The boy heard the familiar voice of his older sister in the morning air.

He moved lazily with many an *oof* and *aaah* and other inarticulate sounds, until a bright light pierced his eyes.

Dawn—it was morning.

"It's morning?!"

The boy threw himself out of his straw bed and gave a great stretch.

He sucked in a breath of air that was cold and comfortable. A fragrant aroma of some sort wafted by.

Bread!

It was breakfast.

"If you don't hurry and get up, there won't be any breakfast left!"

"I know!" he shouted back to his sister, then quickly changed into his clothes.

If it was already morning, then he couldn't waste another minute, not another second. Plus, he was hungry.

When I close my eyes, morning comes right away—so why do I get so hungry?

Maybe his sister would know. He wanted to ask, but right now breakfast was more important.

"Morning, Sis!"

"I think you mean *good* morning," she said in annoyance as he came flying into the kitchen (and dining room, and living room—it was a small house). "Sheesh. That's why we have to have *her* look after you."

"Hrk… She's got nothing to do with this." When his sister brought up his longtime friend who lived in the house next door, the boy adopted the same displeased expression as her.

The neighbor was younger than him, but she could do pretty much anything, so everyone treated him like he was younger and made her responsible for him. He would complain to his sister about it, but she would only smile. You would think an older sister might take her little brother's feelings into account a bit more.

"Never mind that, just you eat."

"…Yes, Sis."

His objection was ruthlessly dismissed, and she gestured for him to sit at the table with a wave of a large spoon.

The dishes on the table included bread, still steaming warm, and a soup made of milk. There were fried eggs on the days when the chickens had laid, but it didn't happen that often. His favorite thing was stew, which they could only make when they had killed one of the chickens.

His stomach ached with the delicious smells.

He took up a spoon, determined not to let any of it go cold.

"Hey, say your prayers!" his sister, who seemed to have eyes in the back of her head, said as she checked the soup.

The boy regretfully put the spoon back on the table and clasped his hands.

"O One who is bigger than the rivers and wider than the seas, thank you for granting us the wisdom to obtain this food."

"Right, good!"

It was typical in these pioneer villages to believe in the Earth Mother, and the boy took pride in the fact that his family was different. His sister had learned to read, write, and do math at the temple of the God of Knowledge and was even starting to teach there herself. It was what had allowed them to survive even after their parents died—and for that, they had to be thankful to the deity.

But… the boy thought. He sipped some soup, then tore off a piece of bread and soaked it in the soup before eating it. *Me, I want to be an adventurer.*

It was certainly not something he could tell his sister.

§

"Just be sure to stay out of the Eastern Woods!"

"I know!"

"Come back at noon and go to the temple!"

"I know, I know!"

With his sister harping at him from behind, the boy set off down a path he'd known since birth.

Well, maybe not since birth, exactly…

On his back rattled the wooden sword his sister had recently given him for his birthday. One of his favorite games these days was swinging it around and pretending he was an adventurer. Of course, in his mind, it wasn't pretend.

My party's one short today.

The girl next door was going into town that day. Not fair. Not fair at all.

"Even I haven't been to see town yet." He drew his sword and took a few thoughtless stabs at the underbrush.

"You there, boy! Don't you be swingin' that thing where there are people around, it's dangerous!"

Of course, a middle-aged farmer standing kitty-corner spotted him and called out. He must have been watering his fields. There was a sound as he stretched out his stooped hips.

"…Yes, sir." The boy understood that what he did reflected on his sister, and he obediently sheathed the sword. "I'm sorry."

"Y'be careful, now." Pounding gently on his lower back, the farmer began ambling away from his field, smiling at being on a short break. He came up beside the boy and let out a long breath, taking a hand towel from his waist and wiping his own face. He was covered in earth and dust and mud and sweat, and the towel was quickly stained brown.

"Where's that gal you're always with?"

"Her? She's in town today," the boy said with a hint of annoyance, but the farmer just nodded.

"That so? I see… She's a sweet thing. Maybe she'll get some pretty clothes in town. Savor the anticipation, boy."

"I don't think she looks good in fancy stuff." He puffed out his cheeks. The farmer patted him with a rough, dirty hand. At the sight of the boy, the farmer laughed again.

"Well, wait till y'see her. Keep it to yourself for now."

"Hrm…"

"Say, boy. You go t' the temple at noon, don't you?"

"Uh-huh. Sis says I have to study."

"She's right enough about that." The farmer nodded, then frowned and gently pounded his lower back with a fist. "Actually, my hips are botherin' me again. Tell the monks I could use some medicine."

"Sure. Medicine for your hips, got it."

The boy nodded, and the farmer's weathered face blossomed into a wrinkly smile. "Good boy," he said. "Oh, and boy. You've been told to stay clear of the Eastern Woods, haven't you?"

"Yes, I have," the boy said, cocking his head. Now that he thought about it… "But why shouldn't I go there?"

"What, ain't your sister told you?"

"No. I never asked."

"Them Eastern Woods—" The farmer folded his arms gravely, letting out a deep sigh. "—There's goblins there."

§

"An adventurer, huh? Wonder if they'd really help us."

Down the crude path out of the pioneer village stood a dense, dark forest.

At the entrance trembled one of the young men of the village—though he was over thirty years old.

The one who had spoken held a rusted old spear, but he looked uneasy and not very reliable. It had, after all, been more than ten years since he had gone off to war carrying that weapon. And even then, the battle had ended while he was still in the rear, and the whole thing had come to nothing.

Now anyone in the village with even a modicum of battle experience had been called on to face the goblins, but they were not very well prepared.

"The Guild can make their promises, but I sure wouldn't want to run into any bandits…"

"Me, I'm 'fraid of black magic…"

The whispering voices belonged to two anxious-looking men in their twenties.

They held hand axes made for cutting firewood, restlessly adjusting and readjusting their grip.

"I've heard you can't let down your guard for the lady ones, either, or they'll suck the soul right out of you!"

"Yeah, I heard that, too," a former soldier said as quietly as he could. "There was a young one, over in the silk-makers' village across the mountain range?"

"Oh, yeah, there was."

"Well, she said she didn't want a long life of eating hard bread. She was going to live a rich, short life as an adventurer."

"Left home, huh?"

"Sure did. But you know what, it was really because she was in *L-O-V-E* with an elf girl, a sorceress who'd come to the village."

"Aww, yikes…"

"'Course, sometimes it's the other way around. Girls get taken in or raped by adventurers who come to their village all the time, right?"

"That's enough drivel out of you. Didn't my grandpa say?" The group's leader, a man of twentysomething years who looked likely to be the next chief of the village, spoke with a severe expression. "The only villages that ever survived a goblin attack were the ones that hired adventurers."

"Yeah, but…"

"Or should we send the little devils *your* daughter as an offering?"

"Hey, now…"

"You must've at least heard the story of the traveling merchant whose daughter was dragged off."

The former soldier nodded in agreement as the timid man whimpered that this was not good, that it did not bear thinking of.

"What I know is my gramps isn't wrong. He knows a whole lot more about fighting than me."

"Yeah, but—but they're goblins. We don't have to hire any adventurers, right? If we just leave 'em alone, won't that…?"

"When one or two come along, you can chase 'em off. Goblins aren't such a big deal." Their leader shook his head, still looking stern. "But gramps said when they start setting up a nest—they'll come for our wives and daughters."

"Yeah…"

"But, look. Ain't much hope we can kill all those goblins ourselves, is there?" As the former soldier spoke, the timid man gave a squeak as if he were facing death at that very moment.

"Su-su-su-su-sure, we can't," he said. "Maybe I could chase off a goblin what came to the village, but…"

"Well, there you have it," the former soldier said. "This is how adventurers put food on their tables—let them handle it."

"Tch," the leader muttered, "what a sniveling, yellow-bellied…"

"Now, now, you've got to think of his feelings, too," the former soldier said evenly, shielding the timid man from the upbraiding. "We know you're betrothed to the chief's daughter, and you're set for the future, but not everyone has that going for them."

In the face of this argument, everyone fell silent, including the leader.

The young people of the village were all enthralled by adventurers. They wanted to love women, eat delicious food, live the high life. They didn't want to spend their lives plowing the country dirt. They would sooner fight a dragon. The readiness to face death came easily to their lips, if not to their hearts.

And the young women were much the same. All they could look forward to was becoming one of the empty-headed fools who had nothing but house and farm work to do or serving the god in the temple to pray until the moment of their death. If they were unlucky, they might be attacked and raped by bandits or the like or grow so destitute that selling themselves became their only recourse…

So why shouldn't they rather spend a night dreaming with an

adventurer, or embrace the fantasy of traveling with one? The stronger among them might even want to stake their claim as adventurers just like the men.

"Well, anyone would worry about their own daughter or sister or son or brother."

Pioneer life on the frontier was cruel.

Monsters were forever appearing, but you certainly could not count on the military to come and protect you. His Majesty the king, whose face you had never even seen, was surely busy dealing with dragons and dark gods and what have you.

A temple where they prayed to the gods on your behalf might be built as a measure of support, and perhaps that was comforting in its own way.

And there were taxes. The rain fell, the wind blew, the sun shone. Some days were cloudy. And there were goblins.

If money ran low there was always prostitution or traveling somewhere to find work…and for young people, it was only natural to dream of becoming adventurers.

If that was what they wanted, they could have simply tried to become employees at the Adventurers Guild in the Capital…

But without an education or money, this, too, was only a dream within a dream.

"I sure hope a good, strong adventurer will come for us…"

"You hope? That's why the king spends our tax money to build Guilds. No need t' worry."

"…Yeah."

More pressing than their dreams or money were the goblins that were so near at hand.

The three young men looked at each other, then sighed deeply.

That was probably why none of them noticed the boy sneaking quietly into the forest, all alone.

§

Goblins.

What exactly were these creatures the adults were so afraid of?

The boy had never seen one, so now he wanted to get a glimpse.

Then I'll have something to brag about!

It was the simple logic of a child.

He had heard that goblins were the weakest monsters. He knew, as well, that when one or two had shown up at the village, the adults had driven them off.

If that was true, maybe he could handle them?

And if he could…

I could brag even more!

The boy walked carelessly down a familiar footpath, swinging his wooden sword.

Humans had not made their mark on this forest, and it was dark even at high noon. The trees grew dense; the smells of moss and animals mingled in the air.

He had often been warned how dangerous it was, but today it was especially unsettling. But the danger and the weirdness were why he so often came here to play.

"…Hm?"

The boy stopped when he saw a set of unfamiliar footprints in the place he always went for his games. They were larger than his friend's footprints, about the same size as his own. They weren't a wolf's, or a fox's, or a deer's.

"…A goblin?"

The moment he spoke, the wind rustled through the grass and leaves.

He swallowed heavily. He suddenly discovered his mouth was dry, and his throat hurt.

The boy's palms began sweating, and he quickly readjusted his grip on his sword.

"I-if you're there, then c-come and get me…!"

Acting brave—though he did not consider it acting—the boy tried his best to look the part.

The wind gusted again, bringing a wet, fetid stink with it.

Where is he?

The boy drew in a breath, let it out. Eventually, he began to move again.

He swept his sword about for no reason, clearing underbrush and branches, striking roots.

Nothing happened. There was only the silence of a forest gone quiet.

No one's there?

"Pff, I scared him away…"

The boy wiped his brow with an exaggerated motion and went to dry his hands on his shirt. At the touch of it, he realized the fabric was soaked through with sweat, and his heart was pounding.

He swallowed again, shook his head. He raised his voice as if to reassure himself.

"O-okay, let's head back. Wouldn't want to worry Sis!"

He turned around—and saw a goblin brandishing a club.

"Ee…eek…"

"GORRB?!"

The goblin seemed almost as surprised as he was. It froze with the club in the air.

The creature was about his height, with dirty eyes and mouth. Pale green skin. And breath like rotting meat.

"A g-g-goblin?!"

"GB?!"

His wooden sword, which he had swung reflexively in fright, smacked the creature in the head with a dull *thwack.*

The thought that ran through his head was, *I did it!* And the feeling that ran through his gut was, *Oh, no…* But this was all too late.

"GGGGG…"

The goblin rose unsteadily, clutching his head. There was a dribble of blood. The boy gasped.

"GOORBOGOOROROB!!"

The goblin let out a howl, its eyes afire, and at the same instant the boy set off like a frightened rabbit.

Run, run, run, run. Stumbling, nearly falling, actually falling, scrambling back to his feet he ran. He didn't even know if he was heading out of the forest or deeper into it. Once he was off the footpath, there was no way to tell which direction he was going in these woods.

"Ergh…ahhh…!"

He was out of breath. He was gasping for air. His throat stung. His whole body ached. His feet were heavy. But he ran.

There was no time to look back. He did not hear the goblin's voice, but it might have been because of the ringing in his ears.

"Oh! Wh-where…?!"

The boy had arrived at a place he had never seen.

A clearing, right in the middle of the forest. Had it always been there?

And not only that—to think there would be a cave!

Desperately sucking in air for his spinning head, the boy crawled into the underbrush. It was not out of any intent to hide. He simply couldn't move another step.

His breathing was faintly audible as he struggled to get it under control.

Then…

"——?"

He heard bold, nonchalant footsteps.

He peered out in the direction of the sound, then clapped his hands over his mouth to quiet the "Oh!" that escaped him.

Goblins.

Two of them—and neither had a wound on his head. Did that make three, then?

"GORBBRB…"

"GROB! GBRROB!"

They jabbered to each other, swinging the clubs in their hands, then shared a foul laugh.

The boy could not understand their language, but he could guess what they were saying.

Because he himself had said similar things—to warm up when there was a fight brewing.

They're going to the village!

He had to warn everyone.

His feet moved without his realizing it. And when his feet moved, the underbrush rustled.

"GBRO…?"

Too late.

The goblin's hideous yellow eyes turned toward the bush where the boy was frozen.

A stubby finger pointed, and the other goblin gave a hissing, evil cackle.

One step, another. The two goblins approached.

The boy's teeth chattered. Somehow, he managed to grab his wooden sword. He had to run. He had to…

But how?

"GBOROBR?!"

The next instant, a sword emerged from the throat of the farther goblin.

"GORB?!"

The other goblin turned toward his companion's cry.

Just behind the creature clawing at the air, spurting blood as he fell, the boy saw him.

He was—he had to be—an adventurer.

A cheap-looking steel helmet. Grimy leather armor. A small, round shield was affixed to his left arm, and he held a sword of a strange length.

He was nothing like the glorious adventurers of fantasy or the boors who sometimes visited their village.

And yet he was, without doubt, an adventurer.

"That's one."

The voice was low and dispassionate, almost mechanical. The boy wasn't sure how it had reached his ears.

The other goblin was bewildered. The monster looked first at the club in his hand, then at the adventurer, then at the entrance to the cave.

And he set off running for the entry.

Revenge, anger, and fear drove him to make for his companions.

In that span, the adventurer pulled his sword from the corpse of the dead goblin.

"Two."

He raised it and threw.

"GOROB?!"

The goblin pitched forward, writhing, with the blade piercing his spinal column—though the boy did not yet know what a spinal column was.

Finally, the creature on the ground twitched again, then lay still.

"Hrm."

The adventurer gave a low grunt and walked up to the two bodies with bold, nonchalant steps.

He yanked out the sword, brushing strands of gray matter off it, then clucked his tongue and tossed it away.

Instead, the boy watched him take something like a dagger from the belt of one of the goblins…

"Oh…!"

No— You can't— There's more— The words came pouring from him all at once.

"There's still another goblin out there!"

The adventurer's reaction was too quick to see. He spun, raised the dagger, and took aim, all in a single motion. There was a whistle of wind, a half-formed scream, and a thump of something heavy falling to the earth.

"GBOROB?!"

The goblin from earlier was behind him, not far away, sputtering and choking on the blood pouring from its throat.

"Oh…!"

Only then did the boy realize how close he had been to being killed himself.

The wooden sword slipped from his shuddering hand, clattering to the ground at his feet.

"That's three, then."

Crushing grass and pushing aside the bushes, the adventurer strode closer. His beat-up leather glove picked the wooden weapon up off the ground, then held it out to the boy.

"Huh? Ahh…?"

"Sorry." As the boy vacantly took the sword, the adventurer continued, quietly and dispassionately, but unmistakably. "Thanks for the help."

He headed into the cave without a glance behind him, and the boy watched him go.

©Noboru Kannatuki

§

"Why, you—! And after I told you all those times not to go into the woods!"

"I'm really sorry, Sis!"

He had rushed to the temple and tried to cover for himself, but his sister soon found out everything. After all, there was no other place he could play that would have left him so covered in scratches.

She dragged him by the ear all the way home where he endured a storm of lectures, some first aid, and then dinner.

The salve she used stung terribly. She wrapped him in bandages, and finally gave him a good smack that sent the boy jumping a foot in the air.

Honestly, he wished she would be just a little kinder to him, but he couldn't tell her that.

"Heavens and all. You always say, 'I know, I know,' but you don't know anything."

These little comments went on all the while they were eating, until at last his sister gave a long sigh.

"Anyway…at least you weren't seriously hurt."

Then she smiled with relief.

I really worried her.

The boy felt a pang in his chest at the thought.

"Um…what about the goblins?"

"Don't worry about them. That adventurer got rid of all of them."

His sister smiled as brightly as the sun, then scowled and pointed to his bedroom.

"That means there's nothing to keep you up at night—so go to sleep! Your friend will be back tomorrow, right?"

"Oh, yeah!"

The boy jumped out of his chair, but with his hand on the bedroom door, he turned.

"Good night, Sis. And…I'm sorry."

"Good night, yourself… Just don't do anything else dangerous, okay?

"…Sure."

He opened the door, closed it behind him, and went into his room. He exhaled.

It really had been some day. He had been chased by goblins, attacked by them, and scolded by his sister.

But…

Snuggled into his bed, the boy turned over until he was looking at the wooden sword on the wall.

He had hit a goblin with that sword. An adventurer had picked it up for him.

The lingering nervousness and excitement of that moment still made his heart pound.

"I wonder…what his face looks like."

I met a real adventurer!

No—that wasn't all.

I helped a real adventurer and beat some goblins!

Now that was something he could brag about.

It was way cooler than buying some fancy clothes in town.

Satisfied with the outcome of his adventure, the boy closed his eyes, eager for the next day to come.

CHAPTER 3

Of the Tavern Waitress

"Hello, welcome!"

"Heyo. Get us three ales and two lemon waters for starters!"

"Certainly!"

"And, uh…eh, fritellas will do. For five!"

"Sure thing!" the waitress responded brightly, glancing at the adventurer with the two-handed sword across his back and noting the number of fingers he was holding up.

Any tavern would be lively in the early evening, but at the Adventurers Guild tavern, it was different. There were people relaxing after an adventure where they fought for their lives. Others could put themselves at ease at long last as friends returned from far away.

Some customers were adventurers from afar, starting with a meal now that they had arrived in this town.

The padfoot, or beast-girl, waitress rushed from one place to another—she loved this atmosphere. The sense that she was helping people motivated her even more than her salary.

As her long, carefully bound hair swayed like a tail (her real tail was under her skirt), she called to the kitchen.

"Three ales, two lemon waters, and five plates of fritellas!"

"You got it. Nice, big order—makes it easier on me!"

A pudgy, middle-aged rhea moved constantly back and forth across the smallish kitchen.

Pots and pans, knives and skewers, ladles and rolling pins. He wielded fire and cooking implements like magic, and the food was ready in no time flat.

A faintly sweet sauce covered the chicken and fish fried golden in oil. They were crunchy and hot on the outside, and when you bit into them, the juices flowed into your mouth. Padfoots weren't the only ones sniffing the air at the fragrant aroma.

"There y'go. Take it away!"

"Yes, sir!"

When it came to cooking, there was no race as accomplished as the rheas.

Of course, I added my own little touch!

Her little touches plus the chef's sheer skill made them, essentially, unparalleled heroes of food.

She drew some ale from a barrel, squeezed a lemon over some well water, and the order was ready.

She pattered over with the meal on a tray to where the party was already seated at a table and waiting eagerly.

Maybe they didn't want to just leave their armor on until they got home, because each of the party members had removed some of their equipment. That the front-row members nonetheless kept their swords where they could draw them at any time spoke to their long experience.

"Thank you for waiting! Three ales, two lemon waters, and fritellas for five!"

The half-elf light warrior who was in charge of the party's finances handed her some jangling silver coins.

"Thanks. Oh, and grape wine for me."

"Sure, I know!"

The waitress took the coins in a meaty hand and put them in the pocket of her apron. They came to a bit more than the amount of the bill—perhaps he was thoughtfully including a tip. Although it was also possible that he was just a philanderer.

"Look, when you go to a tavern, you're supposed to start with ale, right?" a female knight said as if she couldn't believe what she was hearing. She rested her chin on her hands.

"There goes our Lady Knight, saying whatever she will again—always good and true to Order!"

"Well, obviously. It's even written in the Scriptures of the Supreme God," Female Knight said as if she couldn't believe it, puffing out her chest.

Light Warrior pressed a hand to his brow as if to stave off a headache and sighed deeply.

"Kids, just don't grow up to be like her, okay?"

"Yessir!"

"But she looks so cool when she's all decked out, though…"

Scout Boy raised his hand in affirmation, while Druid Girl gave a troubled sigh.

Female Knight puffed out her cheeks, incensed.

"What are you talking about? I always look cool."

"Gah! You haven't even had a sip and you already sound soused." Heavy Warrior made a shushing motion like he was scolding a baby, then raised his mug of ale. "Now, we have to toast! We're back from an adventure. Eat and drink all you like, kids!"

"Wooh! Meat! Meat!"

Scout Boy and Female Knight gave a cheer and threw themselves at the food and drink. Their companions watched them with mild exasperation but set to their own meals, as well.

"Finally home…"

"So we are. Good, work, today?"

"You bet! Good work."

With a jangle of the bell above the door, the next ones to enter were a hale and hearty man carrying a spear and a beautiful, voluptuous woman.

Spearman and Witch slid down into their seats, their faces flush with the satisfaction of a job done.

"Hey there, miss! We'd like to order!"

"Yes, sir! Welcome back!" Padfoot Waitress hurried over to their table, as Spearman languidly raised a hand into the air. "What'll it be?"

"For me… Let's, see. Grape wine and, duck, sauté. Can I get, those?"

"Me… Leg of beef—on the bone and plenty grilled. And apple liqueur."

"Oh, apples..." Witch murmured, narrowing her eyes. Her lips opened the little with a touch of longing, but immediately closed again.

Spearman gave an indifferent shrug. "You want some?"

"Not, necess—"

"Throw in a couple of grilled apples, then. I want one, too."

"...Hrrrm."

"Sure thing, I've got your order."

Despite appearances, they could actually be pretty cute. That was the impression Padfoot Waitress got from Witch, who sat pursing her lips like a little girl.

Or is it because he's here?

"Say, miss?" said Spearman.

"Yes?"

"Is Guild Girl still here?"

So much for her impressions of them.

Padfoot Waitress found her strength leaving her, but she held herself up, facing Spearman, who wore a serious expression.

She pushed her bangs aside and let out a breath. She was pretty sure Guild Girl was still working. The waitress knew well how late she sometimes stayed.

"...Yeah, it looks like she's still here."

"Yesss!"

Witch and Padfoot Waitress watched Spearman without enthusiasm as he made a fist and cheered.

Gosh, and when he has such a gorgeous woman right next to him... was a comment she had better keep to herself.

It was everyone's own business who they fell in love with.

And yet, to think that "the frontier's strongest" adventurer, someone whose skill with the spear could have put the Knights of the Capital to shame, would be this way...

He would look cooler if he kept his mouth shut.

She felt a bit uneasy as she considered that perhaps, if you learned everyone's real reason for becoming an adventurer, it would be just as disillusioning as this.

Well, I suppose he's easy to make friends with, if nothing else.

That was undoubtedly better than to be too aloof—wasn't it? With that thought, Padfoot Waitress scuttled off toward the kitchen.

"Grape wine, duck sauté, leg of beef on the bone, well done, apple wine. And two grilled apples!"

"You got it! Take 'em the drinks first!"

"Yessir!"

Rhea Chef called out in a voice that belied his diminutive size. Padfoot Waitress responded with a shout to match.

When she brought the two their drinks, they offered her a smile and a "thank you," and handed her the money.

"All right then, here's to our 'date.'"

"Yes. Bottoms, up."

As if in harmony with the elegant clink of their glasses, the bell jangled again.

"S-so tired..."

"Come on, walk right! Geez!"

Two young novice adventurers came in, the very picture of fatigue and exhaustion.

Apprentice Priestess all but flung Rookie Warrior into a seat, then wiped the sweat from her forehead.

"Somehow I j-just don't feel like eating..."

"Well, too bad! You have to eat!"

Suddenly, the girl looked up from scolding the boy, who seemed ready fall asleep at any moment.

Her eyes met those of Padfoot Waitress, and the adventurer girl blushed.

"Oh, s-sorry. Umm...One bowl of oatmeal, please, and bread for two..."

"Yes, ma'am!"

"Oh, and water!"

"On it!"

She headed over to the kitchen and relayed their order. Rhea Chef raised an eyebrow.

"Sure thing! Take it out with the grilled beef. Hrm, now, where'd that vinegar go?"

"I know, I know. Oh, the vinegar is on the shelf behind you."

As the chef grinned and turned away, Padfoot Waitress pointed to one of the shelves. The chef grabbed a bit of cheese and dropped it onto the plate with the bread, then gave a satisfied nod.

"Okay, I'll take these over, then!"

"You do that!"

She dropped off the sizzling, oily plate with Spearman and Witch and offered them a word of thanks. Then she pattered over to where the boy and girl sat, but Apprentice Priestess blinked at her.

"Huh? Sorry, we didn't order this..."

"It's okay, just eat it." Padfoot Waitress gave a wave of her hand, pointing at the cheese with one hairy finger. "Anyway, someone will be by soon who can't get enough of that stuff, and we'll have to get a new round out. Need to clear out our stock!"

"Th-thank you."

"Nah. Thank *you* for helping us with it!"

Having thus made a successful round of her tables, she went to the wall and sighed deeply.

The lively noise of the adventurers in the tavern threatened to turn into a ringing in her ears.

They were enjoying themselves laughing, shouting, and singing, and after eating and drinking, they would resume their merriment.

"Mm." Padfoot Waitress found it satisfying just to stand there with her arms crossed, watching them.

Then...

"Ohhhh man, am I tired! I want some food and I want to go to *bed*!"

"There were an awful lot of goblins, weren't there?"

The bell jingled again, and five more people came in. At the head of the party, throwing the door open with a bang, was a high-elf ranger. A priestess of the Earth Mother followed her.

"Well, a feast is customary after a battle. To drink, eat, make merry, and then sleep—in its own way, this is a remembrance of our enemies."

"Indeed, but Beard-cutter will be off to hunt more goblins tomorrow, won't you? Bit of a workaholic..."

Next came a lizardman with a solid, heavy step and a well-built dwarf caster.

And then came the last of them.

"Yes," the adventurer said bluntly as he came through the door. Everyone in the tavern glanced at him.

Grimy leather armor, a cheap-looking helmet, a small, round shield attached to his arm, and at his hip, a sword of a strange length.

"We need the money," Goblin Slayer said quietly.

"I'm sorry. If I had just a bit more vitality..."

Then High Elf Archer broke in as if to cover for the disappointed-sounding Priestess.

"Hey, don't worry about it. Just let some other adventurers handle it."

"If there are no goblins, we'll consider it."

"Sheesh, that's how it always is with you." High Elf Archer looked up at the ceiling in exasperation, wagging her ears.

"Hello, welcome!"

Padfoot Waitress trotted up to the entrance, greeting the adventurers with a bright smile.

There were plenty of wild and lawless adventurers, but these folk had a gentleness born of experience—one of them was Silver-ranked.

So it was only natural that she wanted to serve them with a smile.

"Oh-ho," their intermediary, Lizard Priest, said with a roll of his eyes. "How fares milady waitress? Now, I desire to request some cheese..."

Padfoot Waitress let out a giggle at his somber tone. It was common knowledge that this lizardman had become quite taken with cheese in all its forms.

"What about the rest of you?"

"Hmm, I'll have—what was it?—the thin stuff. Pasta? I'll have that," said High Elf Archer.

"Oh, um, s-something kind of light for me...," mumbled Priestess.

"'S all this, then?" said Dwarf Shaman. "Am I the only one with a proper appetite? Meat, I say, meat! And a good, strong wine."

"Something with meat, yes, sir!" Lizard Priest chimed in.

The hem of the waitress's skirt billowed slightly as she turned to look at the final adventurer.

"Sir, our special today is the pike! Caught in the water town and grilled fresh!"

Just the right ingredients, perfectly done, and of course, the chef's talents were beyond question. She informed him of all this like a challenge, sticking out her average-sized chest as if to provoke a response.

"So what will it be?"

It was a bit of an impertinent way to talk to a customer, but she did not regard this man as a customer at the moment.

She stared at him, refusing to let him get away, and she thought she could see a red eye within his helmet.

"Nothing," Goblin Slayer said. "I'm fine for today."

§

"What's *with* him? Is he crazy?!"

"Well, I don't know about that..."

Padfoot Waitress cut off the workshop apprentice's response by slamming her fist on the counter.

"I mean, adventurers are supposed to kill dragons and drink wine and laugh like *Fwa-ha-ha-ha!* That's their job, isn't it?"

"I won't deny there are some like that." The apprentice accepted the girl's argument with an ironic smile, then stuck a fork in some fish on a plate. The well-done pike had started to cool a bit, but it was still fatty and delicious. It had lemon or some other seasoning on it, giving it a faint citrus smell that made his mouth water.

"Anyway, thanks for the snack. Mm, that's good. Been a while since I've had fish."

"I just didn't want to waste the stuff that went cold. Don't get the wrong idea!"

"I like how you're not even saying that to cover your embarrassment or something."

When had it become part of Padfoot Waitress's daily routine to bring some food—really leftovers—like this?

It had been late at night, all the adventurers gone to their inns, and she was out of her uniform and cleaning up the tavern.

As she got ready to go home, she'd peeked into the workshop, where the apprentice boy was alone, tending the fire.

"What are you doing?" she had asked him, and he had said, "We can't let the fire get low."

Of course, that was just a pretext; with her sharp eyes, she saw that he was making a dagger.

It made sense. He had work during the day, so he had to make time for his own practice.

To Padfoot Waitress, it was an excellent chance; giving him the left-over food seemed the logical thing to do.

"People who can eat, should."

"I think that's a contradiction in terms..."

"That's why it makes me so mad when people ignore my food!" Padfoot Waitress said, showing her anger by flicking her tail vigorously. It wasn't clear how well the apprentice understood the uniquely padfoot gesture.

"Do you understand that this has to do with my honor as a waitress? Or not? I wonder if you even follow my logic!"

"Well..." The apprentice scratched one cheek with a fingertip in embarrassment. "...I guess I wouldn't like it if the weapons I made were tossed just any old where."

"I thought not."

"That guy just throws swords every which way," the apprentice grumbled. And the unfortunate blades were not even the work of the apprentice—he didn't yet have permission to display his work in the store—but of his boss.

"The boss says, 'You're the only one who can be truly satisfied with your own work.'"

"Well, I want to get that weirdo to try the food at our tavern."

"It's not like he doesn't eat, is it?"

"That's just it!" Padfoot Waitress slumped across the workshop's counter, which was polished to a shine. It pushed against her chest, such as it was, and the apprentice boy averted his eyes as casually as he could. "After his adventures, he usually doesn't."

"I—I guess I've heard of people who don't eat before they go..."

"Awww, heck. Maybe he doesn't like our menu..."

"This is really bothering you all of a sudden." The apprentice's eyes crept downward, and he hurriedly raised them again. His cheeks flushed. "What's the matter?"

"I mean, he never used to come to the tavern, right?" she said, apparently unaware of his slipping gaze. "How long has he been here, anyway?"

"About five years, maybe?"

"I don't know..."

To Padfoot Waitress, the question of which adventurer had appeared when was trivial. If one paid attention to such things, one would also remember when they disappeared. Once you started worrying about where so-and-so had gone after a while, you were lost. Better to put all your energy into welcoming the people who were here now. She had learned that her first year.

Come to think of it, didn't the receptionist start to perk up around five years ago?

Padfoot Waitress lay there, her chest on the counter, muttering, "Hmm..."

The apprentice boy tried to keep from looking at her, but somehow kept glancing in her direction. His eyes would travel right, then left, again and again, until before long they had focused on a single point.

"Oh!"

"What?" Padfoot Waitress bounced up, her ears twitching.

"I don't know if it's true or not," the apprentice boy said with a nod, "but I heard once that he likes stew. Beef."

§

"Beef stew, is it?"

"Right!"

Stationed in front of a large, bubbling pot, Padfoot Waitress stuck out her chest, such as it was. Next to her, the chef stood on a stepladder to peer into the pot, crossing his arms and murmuring, "Hmm."

"Sorry, Pops. You having to teach me and all."

"Well, if you learn to cook, I can rest a little easier myself."

"Aw, stop sounding your age, Pops."

"I suppose maybe it is my age talking. I'm like butter spread too thin."

"You mean your spirit?"

"It's like I've been stretched and pulled." With a "pardon me," the chef took a spoonful of the stew and tasted it. "Mm, not bad. Let it simmer a little more."

"All riiight!"

This would be her key to victory.

The chef glanced at Padfoot Waitress as she let out a full-throated "Yay!" and muttered:

"But I wonder how an adventurer will take it..."

"Huh?" She froze instantly. "Was it not good?"

"Ehh, I wouldn't say that." Although if he said anything, he might never stop. Rhea Chef scratched his round nose. "Well, give it a think."

"...Darn it all. You'll rue the day you gave me time to think!"

"Har har! Keep at it."

Padfoot Waitress glared at her boss through half-open eyes as he waved his hand at her, then she returned her attention to the stewpot.

Staring intently at it was not the way to figure anything out, and yet...

"Oh, my, I thought I smelled something good in here..."

She heard a familiar voice and two sets of footsteps. The bell on the door hadn't rung. The newcomers had come from elsewhere in the building.

Padfoot Waitress poked her head out of the kitchen and merrily raised her hand to her two colleagues.

"Hi! I'm just in the middle of cooking. Today's special—beef stew!"

"Oh, stew, that's great."

"Oooh, beef stew!"

They were her colleagues—although strictly speaking, they were officials and she was just an assistant, even though the three of them all worked at the Guild.

But Padfoot Waitress didn't heed such fine distinctions, nor was she nervous with Guild Girl and Inspector.

"Thanks. Huh? Are you both on lunch?" She could see when she peeked out the window that the sun was past its zenith and beginning to sink in the sky. It wasn't quite twilight. "It's pretty late for that."

"We kind of missed it..."

"That's no good, how do you expect to keep your body going that way?"

Or did they "miss" it because...?

Surely there was nothing wrong with letting her sharp eyes turn for an instant to one particular place.

"You're right. I'm famished..." Guild Girl said, holding her stomach. Padfoot Waitress hated that stomach.

We've got to fatten her up.

"Okay, so, would you try some of this? We'll be serving it to the adventurers tonight."

"Of course, if you don't mind," Guild Girl said with a smile and a nod. Then she added, "Oh, but…"

"Hm?" Padfoot Waitress cocked her head.

Guild Girl said awkwardly, "…I wonder what adventurers will think of it."

"Yeah… It looks kind of bloody," Inspector said with a nod.

"Oh…"

Now that they mentioned it, she could see what they meant. The stock, which included tomatoes, was a reddish-black; chunks of meat bubbled up in the stew.

As Padfoot Waitress stood there muttering to herself, she felt a tiny hand smack her on the behind.

"Yeek!"

"'Scuse me, ladies, please don't interfere with my lessons."

It was, needless to say, the chef. The middle-aged man who had popped in from beside them gave his rotund belly an angry thump, and put on a stern expression. "I was hoping to see whether this girl would notice for herself."

"Oh, my, pardon us."

Guild Girl let slip a small giggle and, indicating the stew, said, "We'll have lunch here, then. To apologize."

"So you shall—eat plenty! Is just stew enough?"

"Oh, all right. Let's see, then. Bread and… Could I get some black tea?"

"And plenty of jam to go with it!"

"My pleasure!"

Guild Girl and Inspector made their orders; Rhea Chef gave them a spirited answer and tightened his apron strings.

"Well now, don't just stand there—to work, to work!"

"Ergggg—yessir!"

There was no helping anything now. The food was done, and whoever wanted to eat it would eat it.

Padfoot Waitress rushed around on her tasks, and in due course night came.

When the sun was well and truly set, adventurers poured into the tavern just as usual.

Unsurprisingly, the beef stew seemed unexpected, and takers were few.

Did they not want it right after an adventure? And yet serving beef stew first thing in the morning seemed…

"…Actually, maybe it *would* work to put it on the breakfast menu."

She occupied herself with these optimistic thoughts until finally one adventurer came walking with a bold stride.

For a second, every eye in the tavern turned to him, and conversation stopped, but the chatter was quickly revived.

The grimy leather armor, the cheap-looking steel helmet, the small, round shield on his arm, and the sword of a strange length at his hip.

He walked through the Guild building, heading outside. He did not even look in the direction of the tavern.

As if I would let you get away!

Padfoot Waitress rushed to stand in front of him and fixed him with a finger.

"Sir, today's special is beef stew!"

"Is it?"

"What would you like to order?!"

"Nothing," Goblin Slayer said. "I'm fine for today."

§

"I thought you said he liked beef stew!"

"I said it was just something I'd heard."

It was midnight.

In the scant light of the lamp, Apprentice Boy seemed quite pleased with the tureen of beef stew she had brought him.

This did not exactly offend Padfoot Waitress, but she pursed her lips and glared at him just the same.

"Ooh, potato chunks. Perfect."

"…Are you sure you didn't say it just because you wanted some beef stew?"

"No way. Well, maybe just a little." Apprentice Boy grinned at her.

The well-boiled meat was so soft you could have cut it with a spoon. But it wasn't limp; it still felt just right to bite into. And the juices spurting out each time it was chewed, the oil and soup base, were delicious even if they were a little cold.

As for the vegetables—he did like them chunky and heavy.

"So, what are you doing?"

"I'm collecting the filings from when we did the sharpening."

Padfoot Waitress watched him with genuine interest, and he answered as he gave her back the tureen.

He swept at a corner of the smithy shop with a broom, all the while thinking it didn't become him.

"You get plenty, even from knives." He didn't point out that some people considered swords to be nothing more than oversized knives.

Sharpening was accomplished by grinding the metal against a whetstone the shape of a cart wheel, so the process produced plenty of metal shavings. Making sure these were properly cleaned up was one of an apprentice's various important jobs.

Besides, there was also the fact that mixing them with certain metals would make their material last longer. At times, they also used the shavings when a rush job called for more supplies than they had.

What I really want is to hurry up and do some smithing, though…

As an apprentice, he was still learning. Obviously, no one would trust him with the all-important production of weapons and armor.

So, he believed, he would simply have to devote his utmost to what he was given to do.

It's not as if I don't get it—that feeling of seeing your efforts completely ignored.

What if he displayed weapons he had made—in the future, of course—and they were summarily ignored?

"You want to at least know *why*, don't you?" he asked.

"Yeah, exactly! I can't accept it this way—acceptance is so important!"

"Hmmm," the apprentice muttered, his arms crossed. Then he suddenly uncrossed them and clapped his hands, exclaiming, "Hey, that's it!"

"What is it? Had an idea, O future master smith? Fill me in!"

As Padfoot Waitress leaned in toward him, a fragrance of some kind drifted from her hair. It was the smell of the kitchen's cooking, the grassy scent that was unique to Padfoot's, soap—and something else, something sweet. Apprentice Boy swallowed heavily and waved his hands.

"J-just ask! Ask someone who knows better."

"What, you mean like Pops in the kitchen?"

"No," he said. "I mean that farm girl."

§

"What's that? Stew?"

"Uh-huh!"

It was late morning, at the delivery entrance behind the Guild.

Cow Girl had unloaded the cargo with a "Hhup!" and now she blinked at Padfoot Waitress.

Her generous bosom bounced as she let out a breath and wiped the sweat from her forehead.

Padfoot Waitress was well aware that she herself was about average—actually, maybe a little more than average; certainly not less. But still…

Maybe they're full of milk?

She couldn't keep the sordid thought from crossing her mind.

According to the office gossip, Guild Girl worked nonstop to maintain her figure—in that respect, Padfoot Waitress was still okay.

"I'm sure you're a better cook than I am." Cow Girl flushed and laced her fingers together in front of her chest awkwardly. "I only know how to do stuff you can make at home…"

"It's not about whether or not you're good at cooking." Padfoot Waitress seated herself on a barrel with a catlike lightness. She ran her pen along the receipt she held in a clipboard in her hand. Money matters were the work of the reception staff, but vetting the order was her job.

"I know I ask this every time, but are you sure you don't want to look inside?"

"My nose knows. It's all right."

Padfoot Waitress gave a proud little chuckle and stuck out her chest that pressed against her apron. Knowing, of course, that she could never win *that* contest, she quickly waved her hand to change the subject:

"Like I said. It's not about whether you can cook. There's this guy who doesn't eat, and I've really been stewing about it."

"There's an adventurer who doesn't eat?"

"Is something wrong?"

"No..." Cow Girl gave a troubled smile and scratched her cheek. "...He doesn't mean any harm."

"That's the whole problem!"

"Hmm..." Cow Girl sounded a bit lost at Padfoot Waitress's insistence. She wiped away beading sweat with her arm, then took a seat herself on a nearby box.

She let her legs dangle, carefree, then fixed Padfoot Waitress with a stare.

"Is that all?"

To a human or the like, her tone would have sounded no different from normal. But not so for Padfoot Waitress. Her sharp ears detected the ever-so-slight tremble in Cow Girl's voice.

"Is what all?" She cocked her head, pretending not to notice anything.

"Well, um, you know." Cow Girl couldn't quite get the words out, her eyes darting this way and that. She took a deep breath. "...Do you want to give it to someone you like or something?"

"Ohhh, no, nothing like that."

Padfoot Waitress gave a hearty laugh and waved her hand like she had just heard a silly joke.

"I don't have anyone to cook for besides the customers..."

Her hand stopped moving.

Well, maybe one person.

Before she knew it, her face fell, and she covered it with one padded hand.

There was one person to whom she always gave the food she made.

"...I guess I might give some to that guy at the workshop."

"..."

Cow Girl looked hard at Padfoot Waitress's face. Her frank, light red eyes seemed to pin the padfoot girl in place.

"Wh-what is it...?" Padfoot Waitress asked, but for a moment, Cow Girl didn't say anything.

©Noboru Kannatuki

"...Well, okay, then," she said indifferently after a time, and Padfoot Waitress found herself letting out a breath. "I'll tell you. You have something to write with?"

"Right here," Padfoot Waitress said, turning over the paperwork. She grabbed her pen and said, "Go ahead." Cow Girl gave a helpless smile.

"Umm, all right. The way you make it is..."

And then she explained the recipe in detail.

Stew, really, was a boiled meat dish, not a soup. But the food she described used plenty of milk. And in a word, the impression it made was...

"Surprisingly...normal?"

"Right," Cow Girl nodded with a smile. "It's totally normal."

"I mean, it's just a regular stew, isn't it?"

"That's right," she said, never letting her smile slip. "Just a regular stew."

It was unexpected, to say the least.

The waitress had been sure there was something more...unique to the recipe. She rubbed her temple with the end of her pen.

"Is it some kind of heirloom recipe, passed down in your family for generations?"

"Ha-ha-ha. I guess so, kind of." Cow Girl smiled lightly and jumped down from the box. She smacked her hands to get the dust off, then gave a big stretch, pushing out her ample chest. "Not that I learned it from my mother... Although I wish I had."

Padfoot Waitress tilted her head at the faint murmur.

"Your relatives, then?"

"A neighbor." Cow Girl looked up at the blue sky and narrowed her eyes. The wind ran through her red hair. "The older girl who lived next door."

§

"Hello, welcome!"

"Heyo. Get us three ales and two lemon waters—for starters!"

"Certainly!"

"And, uh…eh, the steamed potato platter will do. For five!"

"Coming right up!"

The tavern at twilight. Padfoot Waitress wove her way through the back-and-forth conversations of adventurers.

It was the same liveliness as ever. The same faces. It was wonderful.

Another day on which they could return home to delicious food and drink. That alone was enough to motivate everyone.

"Order coming, Pops!"

"Sure thing. Try not to let 'em get cold—or drop 'em!"

Such was the favorite rejoinder of Rhea Chef.

She peeked in the kitchen, where soup was boiling noisily, a frying pan was sizzling, and a knife flashed among ingredients.

And of course, the chef was in the middle of it all, his short arms moving ceaselessly.

He does a lot with that little body.

She never got tired of watching him, even though she saw him every day.

When the plates came out, Padfoot Waitress stacked them on both arms, glancing toward the stockpot deeper in the kitchen as she did so.

"Is that okay? It hasn't boiled over?"

"What, are you telling *me* how to cook? This from the culinary equivalent of a five-year-old!"

"I know, I know. I was just checking."

Feeling a lecture coming on, she straightened her tail and skirt and trotted away.

This was always Padfoot Waitress's favorite time at the tavern.

She could welcome adventurers as they came home, see their relief at getting back.

There were those adventurers who couldn't come home, too. She had faith that they were off traveling somewhere.

What happened to an adventurer, and where, was something only the bravest could say…

"…Mmm?"

Padfoot Waitress's ears suddenly twitched. They had picked up bold, almost violent, nonchalant footsteps coming closer.

The grimy leather armor, the cheap-looking steel helmet, the small, round shield on his arm, and the sword of a strange length at his hip.

And at Goblin Slayer's appearance, of course, the tavern fell silent for an instant.

"Sir?!"

"...Reception told me to be sure to stop by the tavern." The steel helmet tilted a little at the sound of surprise that escaped her. "What is it? Have goblins shown up here?"

"Oh, no! Sir, please wait there a moment."

"All right."

Leaving the strange, but nodding, man where he was, Padfoot Waitress hurried off to the kitchen.

"Oh— Oh-ho! What's this, now?"

"Get me a dish, Pops! Just a small one!"

"Tell it to the person who washed them!"

"That was me!"

She snatched a dish from the shelf of tableware as they squawked at each other. She spooned some stew into it, then rushed back into the tavern so she could serve it while it was still hot.

"A taster!"

"..." Goblin Slayer looked doubtfully at the dish Padfoot Waitress slid in front of him. "Stew?"

"That's right!"

"For me to taste?"

"That's right!"

"...I see."

He took the dish reluctantly, but then expertly gulped it down through his visor.

So much for Padfoot Waitress's expectation that he might take his helmet off while he ate. But...

Goblin Slayer let out a faintly surprised "Mm."

The waitress's ears were not as good as an elf's, but they didn't miss that.

She'd done it. A less than gracious smile came over her face as she asked triumphantly, "What do you think? Pretty good, huh?"

"Yes," Goblin Slayer nodded. "Not bad."

"Yeeeesss!!"

She found herself pumping her fist in the air and giving a cheer of victory. She didn't even mind the other adventurers who looked over, trying to figure out what was going on.

"Yes! Awesome! I did it!" She spun around, the hem of her skirt billowing, then said happily, "So you eating tonight, right, sir? What's your order? Stew?"

"Nothing," Goblin Slayer said. "I'm fine for today."

"What?! Why?!"

Padfoot Waitress was so taken aback that she nearly dropped the dish, scrambling to keep ahold of it. Goblin Slayer said, "Someone is waiting for me."

His voice was curt, dispassionate and cold, almost mechanical.

But Padfoot Waitress blinked at the words. She stared intently at the helmet.

In her mind, the red eye gazing back from inside it overlapped with another, lighter red eye.

Oh…

So that's how it was.

"What's wrong?" Goblin Slayer had tilted his head questioningly at Padfoot Waitress, who had suddenly smiled.

She could see it now. Looking at it like this, it was unmistakable.

"Nothing. I was just thinking, sir, you don't mean any harm."

"Is that so?" Goblin Slayer nodded firmly and then said, "Are you done?"

"I guess so," Padfoot Waitress said, to which he predictably replied, "Is that so?" and turned away. "In that case, I will go."

"Sure, good to have you, our treat."

"I don't understand what you mean."

Goblin Slayer shook his head and walked through the tavern with a bold but quick stride.

"Hey, Goblin Slayer! Kill some more goblins?"

"How about you fight something else for once? You've gotta hunt big game like me!"

"Aww, by yourself today? No cute little priestess or sexy elf?"

Replying "Yes" or "Is that so?" and the like to the teasing voices around him, Goblin Slayer opened the door.

And then, leaving only the jangle of the bell behind him, he went out into the town, into the night.

Well, that wasn't exactly accurate.

His adventure over, he was going back. To his home.

"Sheesh. If that was what he was up to, he could have just said something!"

Padfoot Waitress laughed, realizing how one-sided her competition had been.

Then she let out an "All right!" and gave her cheeks a good smack with her padded hands.

The cheer refreshed her, and she retied the apron strings at her back, ready to work.

"Today's special is stew I poured my heart and soul into! Any takers?"

Hands went up. People called out. As each order came in, Padfoot Waitress smiled and wrote them down, calling out, "Sure thing!"

But she had chosen an awfully large stockpot to make her stew. There was no maybe about it: there were sure to be leftovers.

And in that case…

"I can just make *him* eat them!"

If she could make food she liked, how she liked, and feed it to a person she liked, that was enough.

Padfoot Waitress hurried out into the furor of the tavern.

CHAPTER 4

Of a Perfectly Ordinary Goblin Nest

For this goblin, everything was just the worst, the worst, the worst.

They were deep in a claustrophobic little hole that could not be called comfortable by any stretch of the imagination. And he had been posted in front of a door that reeked with a raw stench.

"No! D-don't, stoppit— St-stoooagh!"

He peeked in through the crack left by the ill-fitting wooden door to find his companion smack in the middle of his business. He had no desire to see another goblin's dirty little behind, but the behind of the female who was presently being held down, kicking at the sky—that he did want to see.

"…? GROB! GBROOB!"

But the other goblin noticed him watching and screeched at him, whereupon he quickly turned back around.

This was how it always was. *You're the sentry, so stand guard*, they would say, and he would be left to wait for his turn. They could at least let him watch.

Those were the thoughts that ran through his head as he scrutinized the spear he was holding. It had a metal tip and an oak wood shaft, but the shaft had been viciously snapped halfway down.

It was the goblin who had broken it. He had felt it was too long and too heavy to use, and if he broke it, then he would have two spears.

The weapon had been practically shiny when he got it, but now point and shaft were covered in a crimson grime.

He had been happy when he had received the job of sentry along with the spear they had taken from this woman, but…

"GBBORB…"

He didn't have the slightest idea how he was supposed to get this stain off. Now that he thought about it, maybe the nice, neat belt that other goblin had gotten would have been better. That goblin had such a fine belt yet had the gall to steal glances at this spear.

He could barely stand it. That belt suited him more than that other goblin! Yeah. No belt would fit that lout.

He's part of my family, so if he died, I could have it.

In a horde, almost everyone was related by blood, but that didn't cross his mind. His shortsighted little brain begin fuming at the thought of something he couldn't have.

"E-eeeeyaaaaaghh!"

Like the female.

Each time he saw the others enjoying themselves, doing as they pleased with her, jealousy burned in his heart.

He had been left in the nest on the justification that he was the sentry, and he had never gotten to have one of their catches to himself. He had been part of a group on several occasions, but had never sampled the unique pleasure of being alone.

The woman in that room was typical: struggling and fighting and refusing to give up, no matter how long it went on. Of course, the goblins were doing what they typically did in the face of such a show of contempt—hurt her, break her.

There was one who seemed to have given up, curling into a little ball and waiting for the storm to pass. But then she had died as they had fun trying to find out just what it would take to make her scream.

There were others who apologized profusely to the goblins, kowtowing and scraping their heads against the ground and thrusting their behinds out.

And once, because goblins would do anything, they had cut off someone's arms and legs one by one, boiled, and eaten them.

Now, that was tasty.

He couldn't quite remember when or where that had been, but he licked his chops.

That was, ultimately, the relationship between goblins and other races. If the latter were strong, the former had no choice but to cringe and obey them. But if a creature was dying before them—be it an ogre or a demon—they would be upon it en masse and devour it in every sense of the word. That was how goblins were.

"GOBRBOB…"

"GBORB?!"

His companion, having finished his business, opened the door and came out. Maybe it had given him some nerve, because on the way by he gave a mocking snigger.

This companion thought "guard duty" just meant walking around the nest, and here he was laughing at the sentry. It made the sentry so angry that he gave the other goblin a jab in the butt with the shaft of his spear.

"GOBORB?!"

The sentry guffawed as the other goblin jumped into the air. His victim came at him with fists raised, so he turned the spear around and offered the point.

"GROB! GBOOROBO!!"

In other words, this was his post, so if the other goblin had no more business there, he should be on his way.

The other goblin had no comeback to the authority of a job assigned. As he walked away grumbling, the sentry spat out, *Serves you right*, and smirked.

Now for the fun part.

The sentry glanced left and right, making sure no one could see him, then snuck in through the rotting door.

"GBOB…?"

The female stared upward, offering only a weak "ahh" or "ugh" even when he kicked her. You could barely tell whether she was alive or not. The goblin gave her a gentle jab with his spear, and she immediately cried out, "Gaaah!" He followed up a couple of times more, and she produced some interesting "yaaargh" type sounds.

Bah. Without perks like this, it would be impossible to put up with the difficult sentry work. It was annoying, though, that they warned him not to let her die.

They would be angry with him if she were to die when they still wanted more fun with her. But a little anger in exchange for someone like this? It would be worth the trouble.

"Give it… Give it back…!"

"GRRORB!"

The goblin cocked his head at the woman, who had finally begun to sniffle and sob.

Hmm, this spear did belong to this female, didn't it?

The spear, like the woman, would not last very long. He found the thought oddly funny and let slip a chuckle.

He had his fun with the female until she could no longer make a sound, and then he wandered out into the nest.

He had made sure she was still alive—still twitching, at least—and even taken care of toilet duty.

And it would soon be "morning." Adventurers only came at "night."

No one can get on my case for anything.

Goblins always take things in the way that looks best for them.

"GOROB! GOOBORROB!!"

"GBBROBOG!!"

He had been walking around the nest for a while when he heard high-spirited cackling.

It was the scouts.

Two or three of them were sitting together, drinking wine from a chipped bowl.

They were the ones who searched the roads or the village outskirts for unwitting prey, venturing out in ones or twos. So it was only natural that they got plenty of fringe benefits.

It was not uncommon for them to fall back early to a place the goblins believed was safe, to enjoy themselves. They were always gleefully pocketing the items they had stolen from whoever they'd found. But their job was easy, ganging up to attack their prey. The sentry worked so hard all the time, and *these* guys…!

What about guard work?! he thought, indignant at being ignored. He tried to show them the blunt end of his spear, but they only glared at him.

"GOBOR…?"

"GOROBOR!"

They hadn't done anything to him, and all the spear-waving in the world wouldn't change that. He dodged the scout who made to give him a blow with the bowl, slunk away.

Pfah. They were disgustingly violent creatures. They should just go ahead and die.

Still wracked with bitterness, he arrived at the side path that extended from near the entrance. It was an ambush route the goblins had dug, familiar as they were with earth and soil. Adventurers, or whatever they called themselves, never seemed to think they might be attacked from behind.

There were, of course, rocks nearby to hide behind, and it was one of those that the sentry now approached.

All of it, everyone.

He hated, hated, hated everything.

He hated sentry work.

He hated that he got nothing but a spear.

He hated the scouts for intimidating him.

He even hated their half-witted chief, who had nothing but his size to recommend him. He himself would make a better chief than that idiot!

He could have all the adventurers and village females he wanted, all to himself.

He could make the guards and the scouts do all the unpleasant, annoying things. He would just bellow orders deep in the hole and gorge himself on food and females.

Hrm. Chief sounded like a pretty good job.

He became completely absorbed in what to him seemed a realistic possibility, when objectively it was pure fantasy.

How would he assassinate the chief who had united the horde? How would the lowly triumph over the high?

He conceived a plan that he had no doubt would succeed. Then he slowly raised himself from the shadow of his rock.

But…

"GORB…?"

Suddenly his none-too-sharp ears picked up the sound of bold footsteps.

They were quickly approaching. He hurriedly concealed himself behind the rock, then carefully peeked out, just his eyes showing.

An adventurer!

There was no mistake. Only an adventurer would walk through their nest with a torch in hand.

And all alone, no less. The smell was hard to figure out. He hoped it was a female. But even if it was a male, they could still eat it.

The goblin licked his chops, slavering horribly, not bothering to hide the greed welling up in him.

He would attack, drag the adventurer down, tear at it, have his way with it. *Damned adventurer. Damned adventurer!*

But as he hid, ready to leap out with his spear in hand, a modicum of judgment remained to him.

His prey was alone. But even so, goblins were weak. Adventurers were stupid, but they were strong. Even if the goblin ambushed the adventurer here and now, it would mean nothing if he himself were killed.

He could call out to summon his companions, but he would still be the first to die.

He could sneak back quietly to tell them, but there were scouts along the way. They would get all the credit.

What to do?

The goblin stood there, spear in hand, thinking as hard as he could.

He didn't want to die. He wanted to get something out of this. What to do, what to do?

Maybe I should run.

He quickly shook his head. No, that wouldn't work. If the adventurer found he had run, it would beat him to a pulp. And if his companions won the day, the one who had fled would get nothing. Not mating, not food. He would only be able to watch as everyone else enjoyed themselves in front of him.

He couldn't stand that. So he decided to wait for his moment.

He held his breath, careful not to make a sound, as he trailed the adventurer slowly, oh so slowly.

Finally, his moment came.

"GOROBOR!!"

"GROB! GROBORB!!"

The adventurer arrived where the scouts were having their wine.

The instant he did, he pitched the torch in his left hand directly into the middle of the party.

"GORB?!"

"GRBBBROG?! GROBOOBR!"

Wine splattered, and fire spread. Feeding on the alcohol, the torch flame reached a white heat.

Goblins were certainly capable of seeing in the dark, but their vision was still hampered by smoke.

One screamed, one panicked, and one simply did not know what was going on. Each of the three scouts had a different reaction, but all of them were still trying to grasp the situation when the adventurer acted.

"GROB?!"

A body blow with a small shield.

The target, who had unfortunately had his back turned, stumbled face-first into the fire.

"Four," the adventurer muttered, stepping squarely on top of the goblin as he writhed with the agony of the burns.

"GRBBBR..."

"GROBROB!!"

The remaining two caught their breath. Even so, they picked up weapons to strike the rampaging invader.

But they were too late.

The adventurer's right hand flashed as he flung his sword; it crushed the teeth of one scout as it pierced him through the mouth.

"GOOBR?!"

"Five."

The adventurer did not even look at the kneeling, twitching goblin with brains dribbling out the back of his head.

Instead, the adventurer shifted his weight onto the goblin under his foot, breaking its spine and lunging forward as his left arm approached the final scout.

"GBBOORB?!"

The sharpened edge of the shield gouged the goblin's face. A spray of blood painted the wall.

The goblin threw aside his weapon to press his hands to his shattered nose and eye socket, but…

"That's six."

The adventurer picked up the scout's hand spear, which had tumbled to his feet, and pierced the creature's heart with it.

The last scout soon ceased to do anything but twitch and was nothing more than a bag of blood dribbling innards onto the ground.

The adventurer tossed the spear aside as if it were so much garbage and exhaled.

Then he nonchalantly approached the body, stepped on it, and grasped the sword protruding from its throat.

They were fools.

If this goblin had not been waiting behind, watching for his chance, he would never have known, either.

Three against one. True, the scouts had been drunk. But he could see what happened.

That was why his way was better.

The scout hacked blood, giving a death rattle. In his heart, the sentry was overjoyed at the sight.

That'll show you, you barbaric dolts.

There was no hint of compassion in him for the scouts who had been turned into such avatars of suffering.

But be that as it may, he was angry at the one who would come into his very nest and murder goblins.

That was why this was the moment, when the adventurer, tired from battle, had its back turned.

Now!

His companions would soon arrive, drawn by the commotion. When they saw him holding the adventurer down after attacking it from behind, they would praise him. He might even be able to boast of having stood and fought while his companions were killed.

With his heart full of self-interest and greed, he took a giant leap. He brought his spear down, holding it in a reverse grip.

The belly or chest would do, if that was the best he could get, but the arm or the leg was ideal. If it turned out to be a man, all they could do was eat it.

"—?!"

That was when it happened.

He didn't know what had occurred. All he knew was that his attack was supposed to have been an ambush from behind, but the adventurer was gripping his spear with both hands.

The armored adventurer moved too quickly to see.

And in the instant the goblin was trying to decide whether to let go of the spear or do something else, he found himself rammed, spear and all, into the ground.

"GROB?!"

He hadn't considered this possibility.

His mind went blank; he was at a complete loss what to do.

"GBBOROBO?!"

He could not make a proper response in the midst of his confusion.

He felt a terrific pain from the blow to his back, his flesh and bones cried out, and most of all, he found it hard to breathe.

He opened and closed his mouth, and the spear fell from his hand.

There was nothing else left to him. The adventurer had drawn a sword.

The goblin stood with a wobble and began running for the entrance of the cave as fast as he could—

"This will make seven."

Along with the ruthless pronouncement came a shock that ran from his back to his chest, and his consciousness slipped away.

It never came back.

§

"Hrm."

After finishing off seven goblins, Goblin Slayer finally got to take a breath.

You can notice a tail when an extra set of footsteps comes pattering after you.

He drew out his blade and wiped off the blood on the goblin's rags, then checked the edge and returned the sword to its scabbard. It could still be used.

He traced the point of the spear he had taken from the goblin with his fingertip and examined the broken shaft.

Goblin Slayer clicked his tongue, then added it to his belt.

Then he kicked the scouts' hands, breaking their fingers and freeing the swords that the corpses still grasped.

There happened to be three of them. He took the one in the best condition and added it to his belt. This would do.

He scrabbled through his item pouch, grabbing his canteen and pulling out the stopper, then gulping down the contents.

The canteen was made from a sheep's stomach, turned inside out and dried, and it contained a mixture of well water and grape wine.

The cold liquid slid through the visor of Goblin Slayer's helmet, then between his lips, flowing down his throat and into his stomach.

It would do no good to become drunk on wine, but a little bit warmed the body and helped alertness.

"...Didn't see any totems," Goblin Slayer muttered to himself as he plugged the stopper and returned the canteen to his item pouch.

He shook his head gently when he realized there was no answer.

Priestess and his other companions—he shook his head again to realize he thought of them that way—were not there.

They had their plans. They had their health to worry about. They could not always be all together.

Goblin Slayer turned his back to the wall and pushed his visor down. He quieted his breath. He didn't hear anything like footsteps.

Instead, he heard the snarfing sound of a meal being devoured. He could feel little shock waves in his back. It was clear what was going on.

His light source—the torch—still twinkled among the remains of the scouts' revelries. Good.

Goblin Slayer quickly withdrew a bottle from his item pack and flung it in roughly the right place.

The clay container and the wall both exploded at about the same instant.

"GBRROBORRBBBG!!"

Goblins.

A horde of them, a roiling tide.

But the first several who jumped eagerly forward unexpectedly tumbled over.

They must have tripped on the grease all over the floor. The somersaults were just a bit of added humiliation.

"GOROB?!"

"GOB?! GBOROOBOGOBG?!"

They screamed, finding themselves kicked and trodden by their compatriots, who came one after another from behind them.

Worse, they had fallen into the burning torch and were enveloped in roaring flames.

"GOROOOBOGOROOBO?!?!"

"Eight, nine…ten."

The burning creatures accounted for two of these. The other was one who had been trampled until he fell still.

"Seven left. One spear, one sword, one ax, four clubs. Good."

Heedless of the immolation of their nestmates, the other goblins surged forth, anger and greed shining in their eyes.

Having taken stock of his enemies, Goblin Slayer readied his sword and met them head on.

"GBBRBGGB!!"

The first to come at him was the goblin holding a spear—the literal spearhead of the operation.

"Eleven."

Goblin Slayer nonchalantly threw his sword at the creature. It whooshed through the cavern's stagnant air and buried itself in the goblin's forehead with a *thwack*, piercing his brain.

"GGBGGO?!"

As the goblin stumbled and fell under the impact, Goblin Slayer snatched the weapon from his hand.

A longer weapon was not bad. You wouldn't be surrounded. The first thing was to take out whoever had the most firepower.

Had a big one been present, the priority would have been to reduce their numbers, but at the moment he wanted to avoid being rendered immobile on account of a single blow.

That meant his next step was clear.

Goblin Slayer, still gripping the spear, dashed for the depths of the cave.

"GOROOB! GOROOBORG!!"

"GROOB!!"

The goblins, six of them, followed him with pathetic-sounding footsteps. Goblin Slayer glanced back to fix his aim, then hefted his spear.

"This is twelve."

The spear flew, drawing a bow-shaped arc.

It passed over the goblin who had been shoved to the front and slammed into the one holding an ax.

"GOOROBOG?!"

Perhaps it had been pierced through the stomach; an inarticulate scream echoed around the cave.

Five left. Goblin Slayer threw the scout's sword from his belt. He was running out of time, and it was risky to go in deeper. It was time to engage the enemy.

"GOROBB!!"

"GBOR!"

The goblin with the sword self-importantly dispensed orders to the four with clubs.

Of course, this was no show of courage, nor was it a burning desire for revenge.

They were displeased at having seen their companions killed, and they wanted to pound this triumphant adversary. Most of all, the goblins enjoyed beating down adventurers and stealing their gear more than anything else.

"Hmph."

Goblin Slayer took a step backward, then stomped down the first club that swung at him.

"GBOROB?!"

While that monster was trying to free his weapon, Goblin Slayer thrust his sword at the one that leaped at him from the right.

The blade slid in through the creature's jaw, piercing the head at an angle. But it could not bear the weight of the goblin and broke.

"GOOROBOOBO?!"

"Four more."

As he adjusted his grip on the hilt of the sword, he met a club blow from the monster in front with his shield. His left arm tingled. In the same motion, he made a sweeping gesture with the shield and slammed the opponent into the goblin on the left.

"GBOR?!"

"GOROBO?!"

"Next."

While the two goblins were still writhing with the impact, he brandished the hilt of the sword at a creature in front of him. The panicked goblin dropped his club and tried to run, but it was too late.

"GOBOOROGOBOGOB?!"

One blow. The hilt and guard of the sword sank into the back of the goblin's head, caving in its skull, and the monster screamed.

It wasn't a critical wound, but that didn't matter. He could simply beat the life out of the goblin.

Goblin Slayer pounded the creature with his bladeless sword as if it were a hammer.

"GOROB?! GOROOG?! GOOROBOG?!"

Dull thumps and thwacks rang out until finally blood and brains sprayed from the shattered skull.

Goblin Slayer gave a click of his tongue and let go of the sword, then moved his feet to pick up the club he'd been standing on.

"That makes ten and four. Three left…!"

The two other goblins had scrambled to their feet and were coming at him together.

Goblin Slayer dealt with one of them using his round shield, cracking the monster's head beyond the reach of the other one's club.

"Two left."

The difference in body size meant a certain difference in reach. And in a one-on-one fight, there was no way he could lose to a goblin.

A moment later, the death rattle of the next creature echoed in the cave.

"GOROOBOROB?!"

"GOROBOGR!!"

The last remaining goblin, the one with the sword, lost no time in giving a great cry and running away.

Luckily for the goblin, his enemy was heading deeper into the cave. If he ran for the outside, he would probably not be followed. The hateful brightness out there looked to him like salvation.

The goblin felt no guilt at abandoning his companions. It was their fault he was in danger to begin with.

He trod over the still-smoldering remains of the other creatures, running, running, running…

"Hrmph."

Goblin Slayer nonchalantly let go of the brain-soaked club, approaching the corpse that was impaled with a spear.

The ax was still in its hand. He picked it up with a flourish and flung it.

The fleeing goblin died believing to the last instant that he alone would be saved.

The ax tore through his skull from behind, decimating his brain. He pitched forward and fell.

"Seventeen."

Goblin Slayer took a new torch from his item pouch, lighting it from the embers of the one that lay among the remains of the party.

Then he turned back for a moment, even bolder than before, and searched the corpse of the goblin he had killed with the ax.

He was looking for the sword. When he found it, he put it into his scabbard.

"Three on reconnaissance, one chance encounter, three scouts, ten by ambush. Seventeen total. There are prisoners. No totems. No poison," he muttered to himself

How to interpret this? Of course, he heard no answer. Goblin Slayer started to think.

The nest was on a small scale. There probably weren't too many more goblins. And he hadn't taken their leader yet.

"Perhaps a hob is their chieftain."

And yet, he had no sense that a hobgoblin was coming.

Goblin Slayer soon determined what this would mean.

"It's the sort of thing a goblin *would* think of."

He quickly took stock of all his equipment. Helmet, armor, shield, weapon, all good.

He held the torch in his left hand and walked into the cave with his bold, nonchalant stride.

The nest was large enough to house ten creatures or so. It had some branches, but there was a limit to them.

But more than anything, it was the unpleasant odor prickling in his nose that told Goblin Slayer where to go.

He made several turns in the winding path and soon arrived at a rotting door.

"Ah—ouch! That— That hurts—?!"

"GGGOROOOBB!!"

What emerged was a massive goblin pulling a woman by the hair.

The woman gave a cry of pain, but judging from the state of her body, she was in no condition to resist anymore.

Several strands of hair came loose, taking bits of her scalp with them, but it was all she could do to raise a cry.

As it taunted her, the hobgoblin realized there was someone blocking his way. He looked up.

"GOROBB......"

The hobgoblin grumbled something, hauled the woman up, and held her in front of him.

An awful stench wafted from every part of her; blood and waste mingled together and dribbled down her body.

The hob pushed her in front of himself as if to catch Goblin Slayer's attention with her glassy eyes—presumably he saw her as a meat shield.

"Fool," Goblin Slayer spat. "It won't change anything."

The hob's thinking was clear. Actually, any goblin would probably have thought the same in that situation.

As long as he survived, that was all that mattered.

The creature had meant to sacrifice his nestmates and escape with the female.

It was just the sort of thing a goblin *would* think of.

"GROBO! GOBOOROGB!!"

"..."

He assumed it was telling him to drop his weapon, or let it by, or something similar.

The hobgoblin grinned horribly at him, brandishing the hatchet in its right hand.

Goblin Slayer looked at the woman that the creature was using as a shield. He gazed into her eyes. And then he gave a single, small nod.

"Very well."

He drew the sword at his hip and dropped it. The hob's eyes followed the motion.

Goblin Slayer leaped forward instantly, kicking the creature mercilessly in the crotch.

"GGROOOOROOBOROOB?!?!"

The monster gave an unbearable scream at the damage between its legs. Goblin Slayer had, indeed, felt something burst under his toes.

Goblins were always so cocksure. Even though he had never had the slightest intention of quietly letting himself be killed.

"Erg—ahh!"

"GBBRGO?! GOROOBOGOROGOB?!?!"

The hobgoblin threw the woman aside in his convulsions. The steel helmet looked down at him impassively.

Then Goblin Slayer picked up his sword, held it in a reverse grip, braced himself against the goblin's shoulder, and drove the blade home.

"GOOBOR?!"

There was just one incoherent bellow. The sword stood upright in the back of the creature's skull. Goblin Slayer gave it a great twist.

The sword cut the spine with a crack, and the hob gave one tremendous shake and then stopped moving.

"Eighteen... Are you alive?"

The discarded woman trembled. Faintly, lips trembling, she breathed an "eh" and "ss."

"I see."

Goblin Slayer rifled through his item pouch, pulling out a bundled up overcoat. He spread it over the woman, and once it was covering her scum-drenched body, he hefted her like cargo.

The woman murmured something weakly, to which Goblin Slayer said, "I see," and nodded.

"I picked up the spear," he said. "The shaft is broken, but the point remains."

Goblin Slayer walked quietly out of the cave.

A weak, desperate weeping weighed heavily on his back.

CHAPTER 5

Of a Day When He Isn't There

"Mrm…ooh…hha…"

Just after dawn, cool air prickled her skin; she tossed and turned in her blankets with little noises.

Normally she would have expected to hear them by now—but today there was no sign of any footsteps drawing near.

"…Oooh…?"

She was not the kind to have trouble getting out of bed, but without the sounds she was accustomed to, she found it hard to open her eyes.

When she had finally crawled out of her straw bed, she rubbed her heavy, sleepy eyelids and gave a big yawn.

Midday was still warm, but night and morning had taken on a chill.

With many a shake and shimmy, she pulled her undergarments over her healthily plump body, just like always.

"M-mm…just a bit…too tight, maybe?"

Had she put on some weight? Or just grown a bit? Whichever it was, she did not welcome it. It was unfair to her uncle to constantly be buying new clothes and undergarments.

But then, it's no good to use stuff that doesn't fit, either.

Maybe she would make some alterations to the clothes.

With those thoughts in her mind, she opened the window, and the fresh morning breeze gusted into her room.

Smiling in pleasure, she leaned out, resting her voluptuous chest on the windowsill.

It was a scene she knew and liked.

The spreading farm fields. The lowing of cows in the distance. The clucking of chickens. Smoke rising from the far-off town. The world.

"...Oh, that's right," Cow Girl murmured absently, as she basked in the golden sunlight. "He isn't here today."

§

"How about you go into town?"

"Say what?"

Cow Girl turned only her head to look at her uncle. Breakfast was over, and she was piling the dishes by the sink.

There wasn't much to wash when *he* wasn't there. That made things easier, and that was good, in its way.

"I said, how about you go into town?"

She looked at him again. His expression was simple and frank, and he was gazing somberly at her.

"Hm?" she said questioningly, glancing back at him as she took up the plates and dried them. "Doesn't really matter to me. But I wouldn't have much to do there."

"Now, that can't be true." Her uncle was always so serious. He went on without a pause, "Your friends are there, aren't they?"

"Friends, right..."

Cow Girl smiled vaguely. She took some sand from a bucket next to her and rubbed it into the surface of one of the dishes, *scritch-scratch*.

"I guess you could call that person a friend, if you wanted. But I think she's really more like a companion who shares the same values, maybe."

"You should get out and have fun sometimes."

"Hmm..."

Cow Girl made a sound that was neither agreement nor denial.

Checking that the sand had scrubbed all the stains off the plate, she washed it again with water.

Finally she wiped the dish gently to dry it and returned it to the tableware shelf.

"But there's the livestock to look after, the harvest, the stone wall and fence to check on, deliveries to make, and then we have to get ready for tomorrow…"

She counted off the tasks on her fingers—there really was a lot of work. So many things had to get done. Things that had to be done today. Things that ought to be done today. All kinds of things that could be taken care of rather than put off.

Right, Cow Girl nodded, causing her chest to jiggle. "I don't have time to play around. It's a good thing that we have work to do!"

"I am telling you to go have fun." His voice brooked no argument.

She looked at him, taken aback by his sharp tone.

Her uncle was unmoving. When he got like this, his opinion was no more likely to change than a mountain stone. He had spent ten years raising her, and she understood this without his saying anything.

"Huh? But… Um…"

"You're still a tender age. How old are you? I want to hear you say it."

"Um, I'm…eighteen…" She nodded assiduously. "Almost nineteen."

"Then it's not your duty to work from dawn till dusk every day."

Cow Girl racked her brain for some response.

…Huh? Why am I so against going out?

The thought flashed across her mind and vanished. This wasn't the time.

"B-but, what about the money…"

"Fortunately, we're no serfs. Our lives aren't dictated by a lack of resources."

"Well, true, but…"

It was no use. Her feeble resistance summarily subdued, Cow Girl was at a loss for words.

Well, now what? The dishes were cleaned, and she had no other cards to play.

She puttered about the kitchen for a while before finally slumping into a seat across from her uncle.

"You don't have to worry about me." He was kind as ever, as though he were speaking to a small child.

Cow Girl pursed her lips—he didn't have to talk to her that way—but she didn't say anything. Maybe that was itself childish. In that case…

"Go and have some fun." As he watched her, his craggy face suddenly softened and relaxed. "A young girl working every waking minute on the farm? Surely there's some girlish thing or other you want to do."

"I wonder…"

Cow Girl didn't really know.

Girlish things?

What would that be? Getting dressed up? Eating sweets? All of her ideas seemed airy and vague.

Compared to this, tomorrow's weather seemed concrete…

"…All right," she said after a moment, still not sure whether she understood anything or not. "I'll go out for a bit, then."

"Yes, you do that."

"…Right."

Seeing her uncle's relief, all she could do was nod.

§

She had no cart, and *he* wasn't there—it was just her by herself.

She found her pace unsteady even though she was only going to town on a road she knew well.

How did she normally walk on this road? She ended up feeling awfully puzzled.

And then, weaving her way between adventurers and merchants as they came and went, she passed through the great gate and into town.

Cow Girl smiled wryly as her feet began carrying her toward the Adventurers Guild, normally the first place she would go. Consciously overriding her subconscious, she went straight instead, into town, toward the plaza.

There was chatter in the air, merchants' voices, children playing, mothers calling, adventurers chatting with one another. Burying herself in the sounds, Cow Girl sat vacantly on a random curb. She watched a boy and a girl, perhaps about ten years old, run by. She followed them with her eyes and exhaled.

Now that I think about it… "Do I *have* any friends…?"

There was no one left whom she'd known since she was young. She had moved ten years ago, and for five of those years she had been absorbed in only what was before her eyes.

It's a little late to go down memory lane now.

The way she'd been back then, she was lucky he had called out to her as he shuffled along.

There had still been horns on his steel helmet then, and her hair had been considerably longer.

For the five years after that, her head had been full of him. She had been altogether unable to just have fun.

"Oh, but…"

She shook her head, thinking of the receptionist and the waitress she saw nearly every day. They might count as friends—but there were only two of them. Well, two friends could be enough.

Plenty of people couldn't make any friends.

"…I'm pretty well off."

A fat lot of good that thought did her. She smiled feebly and continued to gaze out at the people who came and went across the square.

They wore an infinite variety of expressions. Some seemed to be enjoying themselves, others looked sad. Some seemed lonely, others happy. But all of them walked without hesitation, with some kind of goal in mind. Work, or a meal, or a place to go home to, or a place to *have fun*, or, or…

Not like her.

Cow Girl sat on the curb, pulling her knees in against her chest.

This is a serious problem.

In the end, I don't have a single connection to anything except the farm…

"—? Is something wrong?"

She thought she recognized the voice above her.

She looked up and saw a golden-haired girl gazing at her with a hint of confusion. She had an elegant, slim frame, and was wearing modest hempen clothes, plain and unassuming.

Cow Girl blinked, trying to remember who this was, and then clapped her hands.

"H-hey, you're that priestess…"

"Oh, yes. And you're from the farm, right?"

"Yeah, that's right." Cow Girl nodded and stood, dusting off her round backside. "What's with your clothes?"

Rather than her usual vestments, Priestess was dressed in street clothes; in fact, her garments could have belonged to a girl in a farming village.

"I stayed behind this time, so I thought…I might as well go out." She scratched her cheek with a slim finger in a gesture of awkward embarrassment. "But I don't have any idea what to do."

"Yeah, me too. I know exactly what you mean. Normally I just have to do whatever needs doing on the farm."

Huh. They were the same.

She knew her sense of solidarity might be a little one-sided, but Cow Girl still breathed a sigh and relaxed a little. She had always been outgoing, after all; she didn't feel nervous. And anyway, this was one of his party members.

It would be wrong to say that there was no shadow of a doubt in her mind—but Cow Girl determined to make herself keep an easygoing attitude.

"You said you stayed behind this time? Why's that?"

"Oh, umm, it's…" Suddenly, Priestess couldn't quite finish her sentence; her eyes darted this way and that. Her cheeks flushed red—had her temperature gone up a little?—and her eyes turned to the ground with a downcast look.

Hm? Cow Girl thought suspiciously, but an explanation was soon forthcoming.

"Today is…a bit of a rough day for it…"

"Sure." Cow Girl gave a strained smile and nodded. It was something every woman had to deal with.

It must have been hard on the abashed younger girl to have the information pried out of her like that.

"What do you usually do, you know, when you're not on an adventure?"

"I pray."

Cow Girl knew it was a clumsy attempt to change topics, but the girl's answer was brief and guileless. She more or less fit the image Cow Girl had come up with after seeing her from afar a few times.

"Really!" Cow Girl said admiringly, and Priestess put a slim, white finger to her lips and thought a moment.

"I also read the scriptures, and the Monster Manual, and I train…"

"Gosh, you're the serious type, huh?"

"I just haven't learned enough yet."

Perhaps Priestess wasn't used to being praised, because Cow Girl's expression of surprise caused her to blush in embarrassment.

Hmm…

She decided not to say that she planned to praise Priestess to *him* later.

Despite how he looked, he did care for people in his own way, so perhaps it would be overreaching herself a bit, but…

"…Hey."

"Yes?"

"How about we take a walk?" Cow Girl smiled. "Since we ran into each other and all."

"…You're right." Priestess smiled again, like a small flower coming into bloom. "Yes, let's wander a bit."

§

"Come to think of it, it's still a ways off, but when summer's over, it'll be time for the harvest festival, won't it?"

"Oh, yes. The Temple will be starting preparations for the offering dance soon."

"I wonder who the dancer will be. Thought about becoming a candidate?"

"No, hardly. It carries a lot of responsibility. I'm not ready yet."

"You think? Maybe our farm should set up a stall… We could do something besides just food."

"It's gotten pretty hot already, but fall will be here before you know it, won't it?"

As the two of them walked side by side, with no particular destination, they conversed idly.

The frontier town was one of the farthest pioneer settlements. Naturally, it had many visitors, and plenty of people walking about. But not, of course, as many as the water town or the Capital, so as they went they saw faces they knew here and there.

"Oh, good to see you!"

"Hello!"

Cow Girl bowed, and Priestess gave a respectful nod as they passed an adventurer they recognized. Her circle of acquaintances had certainly grown since the goblin lord's assault on the town.

It's an odd feeling.

Cow Girl giggled involuntarily, prompting a mystified glance from Priestess.

"Nothing, nothing," Cow Girl said, waving her hand, but the smile didn't vanish from her face.

Whatever *he* might say, he was clearly connected to a large number of people.

Not like me, huh?

"...Hey. What's he like? I mean, usually."

"What's he like? How do you mean?"

"I just wondered if he, you know, was a pain in the neck or anything..."

Cow Girl laced her hands behind her and spun around, but Priestess waved her hands and said, "Oh, hardly! He's always helping me and everything. I'm afraid I'm the one who causes all the trouble..."

There didn't appear to be any falsehood in Priestess's words or expression.

Cow Girl smoothed down her ample chest with relief. Relief that he wasn't causing trouble? Or that he wasn't disliked? She didn't know which.

"But..." Priestess lowered her voice and winked one eye teasingly. "...Maybe he's just a tiny pain."

"Oh yeah?"

The two of them looked at each other and giggled.

It was questionable, in some ways, that *he* was the topic they shared, but at the same time, he was easy to talk about. How he could be strange and serious and dense and you couldn't leave him to his own devices. It gave them plenty of fodder for conversation.

"But it's true that I owe him a lot."

Priestess described a side of him Cow Girl had never seen.

How when she had first seen him, she'd thought he was some kind of monster. How he was, apparently, trying to act like a Silver-ranked adventurer. How quickly he was under the table when the party got together to drink. How he was always willing to take guard duty given the large number of spell casters in his party.

That sounds so like him, Cow Girl thought. But she also thought, *He's gone drinking with everybody?*

"And he's taught me a lot about adventuring."

"Like what?"

"Like..." Priestess tapped her lip with a finger. "Chain mail, for example."

"Chain mail...?"

In the back of her mind, Cow Girl tried to picture all the items he kept in his shed. Chain mail was one of his favorite pieces of gear. She remembered him polishing it carefully with oil. He had even shown her how to make emergency repairs to damaged sections using wire.

"But—" She suddenly remembered a question she had had for a long time. "Isn't that stuff heavy?"

"If you tie a belt around your hips or abdomen, it spreads the weight out over your entire body, so it's not so bad." Then she added, "But your shoulders do get stiff."

Cow Girl nodded. That made sense. "It's tough being an adventurer, huh..."

"I wear just chain mail, but I gather that many magic users don't like to wear it at all." The dwarf, for example, seemed to ignore it.

Cow Girl nodded noncommittally at Priestess's words. There was an old tradition that metal interfered with magic—but she didn't know how true it was. She was half convinced it must be superstition, but once in a while there were people who wanted horseshoes to keep away magic.

Magic, witchcraft, and divine miracles were things Cow Girl knew nothing about.

What she was more interested in was…

"Chain mail, huh?"

"Sorry?"

"…Hey, the Guild deals in chain mail and armor and helmets and stuff, right?"

"What? Oh, yes," Priestess said, nodding hurriedly. "I buy mine there, myself."

"In that case…" Cow Girl grinned like a child sneaking away from her parents to play. "How about a little window-shopping?"

§

"Y-yikes…"

And there, in front of Cow Girl's eyes, was underwear.

Or more accurately, armor that was practically underwear.

It was a set that included just a chest covering and a little something for the lower body. Categorically speaking, it might be called light armor.

In terms of mobility, it easily outdid a full set of metal armor.

The armor itself was beautifully curved, elaborate, and solid. From that perspective, it was unimpeachable.

The problem was, it just didn't cover enough surface area.

It was just chest armor—really, *breast* armor—and panties.

There were shoulder pads, true, but that wasn't really the issue.

"Huh? D-do you wear something else with this?"

"No, that's the whole thing." The apprentice boy working a sword along a round whetstone behind the counter spared them a glance. He had been glancing for some time now, in fact, perhaps concerned about the girls holding the merchandise.

"Has… Has anyone actually bought this?" Priestess asked disbelievingly. It wasn't clear whether she noticed the flush in his cheeks.

"Well, it is easy to move in. And it provides a modicum of protection… At least, that's the sales pitch." Then the boy muttered something that sounded like an excuse—"I'm not sure I should really say this, but"—and added, "Some people, you know. They want to, uh, appeal to guys…"

"Appeal? Yeah, you'd probably get some attention in this." Cow Girl picked up the bikini armor, blushing and muttering, "Yikes."

She examined it from the front, turned it around and observed it from the back, ran her finger along the severe angles of the hips, laid it out, and examined it again.

"Isn't this a little too revealing?"

"…We get enough orders to make it worth having here," the apprentice boy mumbled, discreetly averting his eyes.

"Hmm," Cow Girl breathed. "I guess you'd have to have courage to wear something this dangerous. It's basically a swimsuit."

"That's true…" Priestess nodded with an unreadable expression. She went on studying the items on the shelves with great curiosity. As someone who stood in the back row, maybe she hadn't had much exposure to weapons and armor. Cow Girl was as curious as Priestess.

"Oh, this…" Suddenly, Priestess stopped in front of a display of armor. She had picked something up with a smile. It was a helmet.

"Hey, I recognize that."

It was the natural reply for Cow Girl, who was smiling, too. Priestess had picked up a gleaming, but cheap-looking, steel helmet. Except for the horns growing out of either side and the fact that it was brand-new, it was just like his.

Cow Girl peered down into the helmet through its empty visor, then she clapped her hands.

"Hey, what if we put it on?"

"Huh? Can we do that?" Priestess tilted her head in confusion at the unexpected idea.

"The sign says you can try things on."

"Umm, okay then, here goes nothing…"

Holding the helmet with a hint of reluctance, Priestess first took a cotton balaclava with "For Fitting" written on it. She pulled it on, paying careful attention to her long hair, then slid the steel helmet on over it.

"Y-yikes…"

Her delicate body listed to one side; the helmet must have been as heavy as it looked. Cow Girl reached out frantically to support her. The girl's willowy form was strikingly light.

"Whoa, you okay there?"

"Oh, I'm fine. Just a little off balance…"

Inside the visor Priestess's eyes could be seen, still appearing innocent despite the gear. From the slight flush on her cheeks, she seemed oddly embarrassed.

"Heh-heh… I…I guess it is pretty heavy. And it makes it kind of hard to breathe…"

"That's because it's a full-head helmet. It's only natural—the visor's a pretty tight fit."

At the apprentice boy's remark, Priestess scrambled to release the clasps, and the visor popped up.

"Phew!"

Cow Girl chuckled at the seemingly involuntary sigh of relief, and Priestess's face turned even redder.

"Th-this is no laughing matter…!"

"Ahh-ha-ha-ha-ha! Sorry, sorry. Okay, mc next."

Priestess took off the helmet and then the balaclava. When Cow Girl took them and put the head covering on, she caught a faintly sweet aroma of sweat.

Hm?

Was that—not perfume, but how she naturally smelled? *Jealous!* With that thought, she pulled the helmet on.

"Y-yipes… Pretty tight in here."

"Yeah, right?"

Through the fine lattice of the visor, the world was dark, narrow, and foreboding. She sucked in a breath and let it out, her vision wobbling as she did so.

Is this the world he sees?

What did she, and Priestess, and his other companions look like to him? How did their faces appear?

"I can more or less picture it, but…"

"What's that?"

"Mm. Isn't it kind of unfair that he can see our faces, but we can't see his?"

"Ahh," Priestess said in agreement, giggling. "That's true."

"Not that I think he's deliberately trying to hide… Hup!"

She nodded as the apprentice boy said, "Put it back where you found it, okay?" She returned the helmet and balaclava to the shelf.

She let out a breath, her chest bouncing as she stretched her neck this way and that. She didn't think of herself as in poor physical shape, but all the same, armor definitely left your shoulders stiff.

Hmmm… "Say…"

"Yes?"

"Since we're here…" Cow Girl smiled like a child with a prank in mind. "Why don't we try *that* armor on?"

Priestess looked where she was pointing and then quickly lowered her head, bright red.

§

"Aww, man! My country's toast!"

"Too bad… Well, it's not very funny."

"That dragon is way too strong! I don't have the equipment or the skills to handle it."

"But you'll find a way. Isn't that what makes you Platinum-ranked?"

After perusing the wares at the workshop, the two of them turned to the tavern and saw a strange sight.

It was past noon but not yet twilight, and there weren't many customers at the Guild tavern. If anything, they seemed to be just getting ready. The chairs were set on the tables, and the waitress was sweeping a corner of the floor.

Inspector, Guild Girl, and High Elf Archer were seated at a table with cards spread out in front of them. They made strange company, but a company they made.

"What are you all doing…?" Priestess asked hesitantly, blinking as she peeked at the tabletop.

She still seemed a bit agitated and had been unable to calm down yet; she straightened her slightly disheveled clothing.

"Oh, it's a tabletop game," Guild Girl answered, looking back over her shoulder at Priestess. She wasn't wearing her uniform, either, but personal clothes. She made a tidy and fashionable picture.

Thinking to herself, *She looks good*, Cow Girl directed her eyes to the table. There was, indeed, a game board with several pieces, cards, and dice.

"I found it when I was organizing some old papers yesterday, so we thought we'd try it..."

"That dragon, though! It's so strong!" High Elf Archer whined, her little chest pressed against the table.

"If it weren't strong, it wouldn't be a dragon. I understand what you're saying, but take it easy," Inspector—also in personal clothes—said with a strained smile. Presumably, the red-colored dragon piece sitting smack in the middle of the table was the wyrm in question. And the pieces lying on their sides around it were all the adventurers who had died challenging it.

"So how y'feeling?" High Elf Archer asked, swiveling her head toward Priestess.

"Oh, okay," Priestess nodded in embarrassment. "It's about over now."

"Cool," High Elf Archer said, waving her over. "In that case, help me out, here. I don't have enough adventurers anymore."

"There are...adventurers...in this tabletop game?" Cow Girl tilted her head in perplexity. It almost made sense, but she couldn't quite put the pieces together.

"To put it simply," Guild Girl said, "you pretend to be an adventurer. There are plenty of rules and stuff, though."

"Pretend to be an adventurer?" Cow Girl murmured, ruminating on the idea. "So you, like, slay goblins and stuff?"

"Sure. Some more basic ones exist, where you're like a real adventurer searching through a cave." Guild Girl poked one of the metal pieces, perhaps a shabby-looking light warrior or thief, and smiled. As far as Cow Girl could tell, the piece wasn't wearing a helmet. She was mildly disappointed.

"This is from a higher-level perspective, where the question is how you protect the world from danger."

"You have to collect the legendary weapons and armor and make sure your skills are up to snuff before the dragon wakes up," High Elf Archer grumbled, abruptly raising her head and letting her ears droop. "But we don't have enough hands or enough time."

"You can also take quests from the village, and collect gear, and fight the dragon…" Inspector counted off the tasks on her fingers, nodding to herself. She seemed full of confidence despite having lost the battle, which made her appear silly yet reliable. "It can give you a taste of running an Adventurers Guild, where you have to do everything."

"I didn't know there were games like this," Cow Girl said, reaching out with great interest and picking up a piece that looked like a knight in armor and helmet.

He looked a little more ragged, or at least, his equipment looked cheaper—but what a fine knight. Not bad.

"This is completely new to me…"

In her mind, "games" were mostly limited to those where you scored points with combinations of cards. Similar entertainments might include listening to songs, playing dice, and maybe competitions if there was a festival.

Guild Girl chuckled, watching her stare at the pieces and board.

"Want to try it?"

"Huh? Can I?"

"Sure," Guild Girl said, crinkling her eyes and nodding at the way Cow Girl's face lit up. "It's not easy to just wait there doing nothing, is it?"

"Hrm." Cow Girl let out a small sound. There was no besting this girl. *I guess this is what they call an adult woman.*

Whether or not she was aware of Cow Girl's thoughts, Guild Girl never stopped smiling.

"Come on, we'd love to have more adventurers. Don't be shy!"

"Uh, sure, don't mind if I do, then… How about you join me? Since you're here…"

"Oh, okay!"

Cow Girl gave Priestess a tug on the sleeve, practically pulling her into a seat. Now there were five women forming a complete circle around the round table. No doubt many adventurers, had they known about this, would have complained that they wanted to go to the tavern.

"So start by picking your piece, please," Guild Girl said, her voice and smile softer than they usually were at the front desk.

"Hmm..." Cow Girl put her hands together in front of her chest, staring intently at the various adventurers lined up on the board.

Yeah... I think this is the one I want.

Unsure though she was, she took the knight she had picked up earlier. The steel helmet made it impossible to see its face, but it had its shield and sword raised and looked straight ahead.

"For me...I think this one."

"Oh, um, I'll take..." Priestess put a pale finger to her lips and thought, a bit lost as she gazed at the pawns. Then, with an "ah!" she glanced around and chose a particular figure.

"Th-this one, please!"

The character she had selected was an elf spell caster, her voluptuous body draped in a robe.

"Good choice," High Elf Archer said with a knowing laugh, and Priestess squirmed a bit.

"Okay, for me..." High Elf Archer flicked her ears with an expression like a hunter stalking her prey. "Right! I'll take this one this time! A dwarf warrior!"

"Gosh, are you sure?" Guild Girl asked, but High Elf Archer replied, "Of course!" and stuck out her little chest. "I'll show that dwarf I'm better at...dwarf-ing...than he ever was!"

"I'll continue as the scout, then."

"Heh-heh-heh! That means you have no monk. Well, I'll handle that."

Guild Girl smilingly set a light warrior with shabby-looking equipment on the board, while Inspector picked an old man holding a holy seal.

And so their adventurers were assembled. A knight in armor and helm, an elf sorceress, a dwarf warrior, a light scout, and a veteran monk. This was the party that set out to face the humongous dragon and save the world. Guild Girl briefly explained the rules to Cow Girl, who then took the dice firmly in hand.

Here goes.

"My adventurer is the hero who's gonna protect the village, rescue the princess, and defeat the dragon!"

With this resolute declaration, Cow Girl let the first roll of the dice fall upon the board.

§

"Ahh, we lost."

The town and the sky were tinged with the ultramarine of twilight. Cow Girl spoke indifferently, looking up at the stars that twinkled in the distance. As she walked along, hands clasped behind her, Priestess scuttled alongside like a small bird.

"We weren't able to get the Sword of Dragon Slaying, were we?"

"Couldn't get through its scales."

In the end, they had had their hands full with goblin slaying. The dragon had destroyed the girls, and they hadn't been able to save the world, but…

"But it sure was fun, wasn't it?" Priestess said.

"Sure was," Cow Girl agreed.

Autumn still seemed some time away, but the breeze that blew cooler and cooler hinted at it.

The world he saw.

The world he lived in—

She had caught the slightest glimpse of it.

"Hey…" Cow Girl laughed as the breeze caressed her skin, flushed from the game. "Window-shopping at the weapon shop, playing at the tavern… Not very girlish, is it?"

"Ah-ha-ha-ha…"

Priestess gave a dry laugh and avoided the question. She was three or four years younger than Cow Girl, and she seemed like a little sister.

I wonder how he thinks of her.

"Hm." Priestess might or might not have noticed the small breath Cow Girl let out. But she gazed up at her with a guileless smile.

"I'd like to play again sometime."

"…Yeah. Me too."

"In that case…" Priestess ran several steps ahead, *tap-tap-tap*, and spun around to face Cow Girl. Her golden hair flowed behind her head, catching the last light of the sinking sun and sparkling. "…Let's do it!"

Huh. Cow Girl exhaled without realizing it. *I guess I do have some connections here.*

She had thought she had only him, and the farm. But because he was connected to this girl, now she was, too.

"…Sure." Cow Girl dusted off her behind and smiled. "Let's do this again sometime."

CHAPTER 6

Of the Destruction of the Demon-Enthralled Temple of Doom

Riiing. She squinted in happy comfort as she rang her sounding staff. The first wind to signal the end of summer brushed her cheeks. The carriage rattled along. How pleasant it would have been to walk alongside it on the road.

She came back to herself. She had nearly forgotten that she was in the middle of an escort quest. As a member of the clergy, she sometimes felt she could sense the presence of the gods at moments like these.

Only a few clouds dotted the sky. In the distance, a dark shadow flew. A hawk? An eagle? A falcon?

"That bird's quite a ways up there, isn't it?"

"It is indeed…"

The one who had spoken to her was sitting on the roof of the carriage.

The ranger with the crossbow was not, of course, up there for the fun of it. Someone needed to keep watch. Ranger had been trusted to keep an eye on the surroundings and showed no sign of letting attention lapse.

So the suspicion in Ranger's voice caused her to immediately tighten her grip on her sounding staff. Each of the others readied their equipment as well, preparing against something they could not see. The only one who seemed not to notice anything was the carriage's owner, a merchant. They ignored him as he asked, "What's all this, then?"

Ranger said in a low voice, "Don't you think that bird's a bit too large?"

"Now that you mention it..."

It happened as she tried to get a closer look.

It was closing the distance even as she watched: skin and claws, beak and wings the color of dark ash—

"Demon!"

They reacted to the voice of their companion, Ranger, but they were too late to take initiative. In her case, critically too late, and the monster—the stone demon—was painfully quick. It was not fate or chance, but a cold difference in abilities that was her undoing.

Even as she thought *Huh?!* her feet were already floating above the ground. She flailed her legs, but it meant nothing; she was pulled straight up into the air. The ground, the carriage, her friends, all grew farther away.

"Ergh...ahh...ow...eeyikes?!"

She beat at the monster with her sounding staff in her desperate struggle to resist, whereupon it squeezed its claws into her shoulders and shook her.

She looked down and gave a squeak at the height. She felt her lower body grow moist.

"Hrrgh— Eeegh!"

The problems didn't stop there. Her thigh burned like it had been struck with hot tongs. Ranger must have loosed an arrow in an attempt to do something, and the demon must have used her as a shield.

She looked down, her vision clouding with tears, to see their spell caster chanting something.

Stop, stop, stop, stop! She waved her sounding staff desperately, shaking her head *No, no!*

We're wrong! This isn't a demon! It's not a—!

"Aaaaahhh!"

The creature dodged the flood of lightning, whipping her about. The arrow in her thigh dug deeper into the flesh. She screamed and shook.

She shouldn't have done that.

The claws in her elbows slipped, tearing skin and flesh and drawing blood.

"Hrk!"

A sound escaped her. The sensation of floating. Wind. Wind. Wind. Wind.

Oww, I'm scared, help me, God of Knowledge, O God, oh God...!

Sadly, all this might have been a fervent wish on her part, but it was not a prayer.

So it did not reach the gods. Her one piece of good luck was that she felt no pain. She was unlucky until the moment she struck the ground, consciousness never left her.

Although now that she was a twitching lump of ruined flesh, it didn't really matter.

§

"So what's the plan?"

A brusque male voice sounded in the wind-whipped wasteland. The spear he carried across his back and the armor he wore made him look handsome and brave.

In front of Spearman's eyes rose a white tower, sparkling in the noon light. The walls were made of a shimmering white stone; from the way it reached to the sky without a single seam, it might have been ivory. But the thought that there was no elephant this huge left little doubt that this was the product of magic.

"I'd guess that thing has at least sixty floors."

"Walking in through the front door might be tricky."

The answer came from someone no less heroic-looking than Spearman. His muscular body was armored, and across his back he carried a broadsword almost as tall as he was. Heavy Warrior, famous in the frontier town, stretched out his palm and looked upward, squinting at the top of the tower.

"Eighty or ninety percent odds this tower was built by the kind of jerk who would fill it with monsters and traps."

At his feet was a brutally mangled corpse; it appeared to have been dropped from a great height. They had already collected the level tag that had been around its neck, giving its name, gender, rank, and class. Apparently the body had belonged to a young girl, but whether she had died before her fall or because of it, they didn't know.

They saw other crimson dots around the tower, presumably more remains.

"Suppose some weird magical type built it as a hideaway. I'd say he's gone bad."

Heavy Warrior gave the corpse a gentle poke with his boot. The tower's owner was a Non-Prayer—he had forgotten how. Meaning this adventure would basically be a hack-and-slash, full of monster opponents.

"I doubt there is a need for us to face them head-on."

The final person spoke in a low, dispassionate voice. It was a man in grimy leather armor and a cheap-looking steel helmet, with a round shield on his arm and a sword of a strange length at his hip. He reached into the item pouch on his waist and began digging through his equipment.

"We can climb the wall."

"Hey, you mean with a rope or something? If the anchors come out midway, we'll come tumbling right down!"

"Hold a piton in each hand and pull yourself up."

Spearman gave an exasperated shrug, gawking at the piton Goblin Slayer had produced.

"Do you have any climbing experience?"

"A bit, on mountains. Cliff sides, too."

Heavy Warrior folded his arms and grunted. He held out a finger, measuring the tower's height, and clicked his tongue.

"The question is how to fight anything that jumps you on the way up. It doesn't have to be a demon. A gargoyle would be trouble enough."

"Gargoyle?"

"Stone statues," Heavy Warrior said, indicating their approximate size with his hands. "Wings. They fly around in the sky."

"Hrm." Goblin Slayer let out a grunt. "So there are such enemies as those, too…"

"Yeah. Personally, I'm all about melee weaponry, but…a magic user would sure make things easier right about now."

"Don't get all fired up here, huh?" Spearman looked at Heavy Warrior, who had begun formulating a strategy with the utmost seriousness, as though he couldn't believe what he was seeing.

"So, what? You want to cut your way in, detect and disarm traps, search around? I sure don't." Heavy Warrior heaved a sigh, sliding the massive sword on his back to rest between his shoulder blades. "Because we have no spell caster, no monk, and no thief."

At that, Spearman could only fall silent.

§

There was an endless array of places to adventure in the world. Ruins from the battles of the Age of Gods were numerous, and all the more so on the frontier. Whether they followed Order or Chaos, nations flourished and then declined, and the cycle continued with another nation arising. As a result, finding one or two new ruins was nothing to write home about. But when ruins appeared one day that were not there the day before—that was something else.

It was supposedly a passing merchant caravan that had first discovered the ivory tower rising from the waste. The forest that had been there on their outward journey was gone, replaced by the white spire that gazed down on them.

Naturally, their surprise was tremendous, but they'd had no time to stare—they had been attacked by creatures with human shapes and wings like bats.

Demons! Those awful servants of Chaos! Those Non-Prayer Characters!

The merchants scurried away, and via the Adventurers Guild, their report was sent to the king himself. The king could have sent in the military to exterminate the threat, and the matter would have been settled. If only things were so simple.

To send in the army required men and money. In this case, the men were regular citizens, and the money was taxes. Taxes might go up next year. And relatives, family members, friends, and neighbors might die doing their duty as soldiers. The citizens found this intolerable, and it bred only resentment.

And then there was the dragon who lived in the volcano to keep an eye on, and other problems like the partisans of the Demon Lord who still threatened the area. To send in the army would mean there were fewer people to attend to these other matters.

And if the tower was bait, a diversion, what then? True, demons were gathering there, but it was still just a tower in the middle of a wasteland. Maybe some twisted magician had built it. It couldn't be said yet whether it was a threat to the country or the world. There was no reason for the military to get involved.

You might ask, then, what the military was for. To stand ready against an invasion by the forces of Chaos, of course. In the recent climactic battle between the new Platinum-ranked hero and the Demon Lord, they had been on the battle lines. Casualties had been high. Many died, many were wounded. They were in no shape to go immediately to their next skirmish or major battle.

More than anything, simple strategy told that trying to cram an army into a ruin or a cave was a good way to get it destroyed. Army units were meant to fight on the open plain with enemy units, not to go into enclosed spaces that not even horses could enter.

Ruins and caves had monsters in them that were threatening the pioneer villages. How could the army be dispatched to all of them at once? It was precisely because the king and nobles were a good king and good nobles that they could not use their forces so lightly.

"But neither will this matter bear to be ignored."

The young king, visiting his friend for the first time in a long time, sighed deeply.

The place was dappled in soft sunlight, full of tranquil, pure silence.

The plant life was carefully tended, the flowers fragrant. The white pillars in the grove appeared to be massive trees. The burbling of a stream, which seemed to come from no place in particular, was soothing to his frayed nerves.

"What do you think I should do?"

"Oh, my."

They were in a garden in the deepest part of the Temple. Its priestess gave an elegant smile and cocked her head. Her beautiful golden hair flowed like honey, cascading over her ample chest.

"Quite an interesting change of heart for someone who turned his back when we were dealing with the goblins."

"You must understand, though that may have been a personal tragedy, in the grand scheme of things, it was trivial."

The king spoke briefly, then waved a hand as if to clear the words away.

The way he settled into the seat that had been prepared for him was at once uncouth and yet graceful. Was this what they called kingliness? Or aristocratic bearing? Whatever it was, he moved as one who had known it since birth.

"And some goblins can easily be handled by a party of adventurers."

"...Yes. You're right."

That was simple fact.

Goblins were dangerous, and if they defeated you, "tragedy" was the right word for what awaited.

But goblins remained the weakest monsters, and they were not the only ones against whom loss meant a cruel fate. You might be eaten by a dragon, dissolved by a slime, or smashed to bits by a golem...

What ultimately awaited you was the same thing you would find when the goblins had finished having their way with you: death. Whether it was due to lack of physical strength, or skill, or simple bad luck, there was no future for those who could not defeat goblins.

"As Your Majesty is most kind..."

A comic song came from the woman's half-open lips.

Once a king so kind and fair
To take his taxes did forebear
Water he gave to a raging river
And city councils aided ever
Tucked the councilmen into bed
And every starving person fed
He made his soldiers passing bold
And heroes sent to goblin holes:
The Capital soon was a feast for trolls.

* * *

The king frowned to hear a song that made light of the nobility, and she giggled like a girl.

"Is this not the moment to call in adventurers, Your Majesty?"

"Indeed, it may be…"

The king put a hand to his brow, rubbing it as if to loosen a taut muscle, and nodded. He had thought it would come to this.

The army was not suited to monster hunting. Hence they would give those scoundrels status, give them rewards—they would send in the adventurers. That was what kept the world turning. They would just do it again now. Weren't adventurers monster-hunting specialists, after all?

"The merchants said they were attacked by demons, but we don't know for sure what was responsible."

The king shook his head as if to point out that there was no proof, then settled heavily into his chair.

One could hardly have sat on a throne the same way. He closed his eyes, breathing in the refreshing air of the garden to his heart's content.

"I very much doubt merchants could tell the difference between a demon and a gargoyle."

"It's an evil spell caster's tower then, is it?" The woman who was master of this temple gave a chuckling laugh, and murmured, "My, how scary," as if it was none of her concern.

The king lifted his head just enough to glare at her from lidded eyes, but made no further retort. This was how she was going to needle him for ignoring the goblin incident. The ability to accept resentment of his policies cordially was, he supposed, the mark of a king. Let them call him incompetent if they wished.

"This is certainly more dangerous than goblins. But it's nothing compared to the Demon Gods."

"True, indeed."

"It seems some necromancer to the south has found an ancient tomb." The king leaned far back in his chair, almost as if to say the topic bored him. The chair gave a creak. "An army of the dead! It doesn't leave me much luxury to deal with goblins or one lone tower."

"Heh-heh. How very tired you must be." As she spoke, the woman

let her thighs peek past the hem of her dress as if putting them on display.

"Status is a difficult thing," the king muttered. "I can't even meet my friends without a pretext."

"Such is position," the woman whispered. "Everything changes—what you can see, and what you can't."

"I've lost the ability to say that my companions and I should simply deal with it with our swords, as we did in the old days." The king sighed, seeming to chew over a memory of times past. "I can't help feeling things were easier back when I was a single lord challenging labyrinths by myself."

"Ah, yes, you cut such a dashing figure, fleeing after your beating by that bushwhacker."

"I seem to recall a party that suffered a terrible fate when attacked by slimes."

The bantering tone gave way to a more scathing one. Sword Maiden let out a quiet breath. "There are times when I, too, wish to quit my position and go back to just being a girl."

"Does even the archbishop of the Supreme God feel so?"

"Yes." The blind cleric's cheeks tinged a pale rose, and her lips formed a generous smile. She put her hand to her ample bosom to keep it from quaking, and in a voice as sultry as if she were confessing her love, she said, "Lately, very much so."

"Things have not gone the way either of us expected. But that's what makes life interesting." With that whisper, the king made a show of rising from his chair. "It is about time I took my leave. After all, I did only come to borrow a few war priests."

"Yes, Your Majesty. I am happy we had the chance to speak."

"I wonder." The king gave a light smile that encompassed at once the bitter and the familiar. "You sounded like you had someone else on your mind besides me."

§

"Sorry, can't do it."

Heavy Warrior looked at the quest form and shook his head firmly—even though it was signed by the king himself.

"Is it too difficult?"

"Nah, but my party's under the weather right now. Otherwise we would've taken it."

"Well, this is a tight spot," Guild Girl muttered again, furrowing her brow at the grim-looking Heavy Warrior.

In her hand she held a request to investigate the ruins tentatively called the "Demon's Tower."

Recently, it had become more and more common for ruins and labyrinths to appear suddenly. Ever since the defeat of the Demon Lord, his remaining partisans had been doing their dark work far and wide. While the military licked its wounds, evil spell casters and the like grew less reluctant to be seen by people.

As part of the Guild, it would be untrue to say Guild Girl did not wish to assign all the available quests. But even with a reward of dozens of gold pieces per request, there were a hundred or two hundred to be dealt with. She realized the national treasury was essentially unlimited and could think of nothing more indulgent than this.

"We'd be up against demons, right?"

Whether or not he could hear the sigh from her well-formed chest, Heavy Warrior took another look at the quest sheet. With a finger wrapped in a simple glove, he slowly traced the letters dancing on the page, then brought his fist down.

"Without at least one spell caster and a scout… Silver-ranked ones, at that."

"A party of three?"

"That would be the minimum. If possible, I'd specifically like both a wizard and cleric with me and two others on the front row, and that scout. Six altogether."

Hm, hm, hm. Guild Girl thought this over with a serious expression on her face, the papers in her hand rustling as she flipped carelessly through them.

Adventure Sheets.

They recorded how each adventurer's abilities had grown on each adventure they had been through. It would not be an exaggeration to say that in a sense, this sheaf of paper was those adventurers' very lives. The pile contained scads of novices—wizards and clerics and scouts and warriors. But when it came to those who had made it to the upper ranks, the number dropped dramatically. One of their problems was that there were so few mid-rank veterans.

We don't have anyone who fits that bill neatly.

Guild Girl glanced out at the adventurers who made the building so lively. Of course they had to be capable, but they also had to be decent people. After all, the quest giver this time was the king himself. The Guild didn't need someone who was just out to prove something. They could be a bit self-interested, or ambitious, but they had to understand what was really at stake…

"If only there was someone who had all those qualities, *and* could balance magic use and battle…"

"You got it! I'm right here!"

It was like a dream. Her wish had just happened to slip out, but someone responded enthusiastically.

He came dashing up to the counter gleefully, carrying his spear, as if he'd been waiting for this moment all his life. As soon as Guild Girl realized who it was, she said, "Ah!" and pasted a smile on her face. "Come to think of it, I recall you learned a bit of magic."

"An adventurer has to be ready for every possible situation!" Spearman was nodding eagerly and confidently, and he didn't seem to notice Heavy Warrior exclaiming, "Aggh" and slapping his forehead—a gesture that was easy enough to read.

Regardless, Guild Girl knew full well that Spearman worked with Witch.

"Ahem, is your…party all right with this?"

"Oh, sure. We just got back from one of our 'dates.' Think I'll let her rest."

…Is he sure about this?

Guild Girl glanced over Spearman's shoulder and saw Witch behind him, lounging on the bench. Witch offered her an elusive smile.

That's the most problematic attitude of all.

Fiddling with her braids with one hand, Guild Girl let out a faint, troubled sigh. From Witch's perspective, Guild Girl was a romantic rival. But this was business…right?

Hrm. I can't let my personal life get mixed up with my work.

"All right, so for the time being, the two of you—is that right?"

"Sure, I don't mind. I can trust…well, I have confidence in this guy." Even though he seemed to muddle his words a bit, Heavy Warrior nodded. "But it's still not enough."

Spearman snatched the quest paper from Heavy Warrior with a "Lemme see that," and cocked his head. "How are we not enough?" he said.

"I want a scout, at least."

"Not a lot of talented scouts out there. What about that kid in your group?"

"I don't want to drag him off to fight some demons," Heavy Warrior said gravely. "I couldn't take the responsibility." He glared at Spearman. "I don't necessarily need someone of good alignment, but I want at least neutral."

With alignment, "good" and "evil" did not quite have their literal meanings, but rather described whether one was other-centered or self-centered, whether they preferred fighting or not. Scouts and thieves were often out for themselves and willing to take action. It was something worth thinking about if you didn't want to have to worry whether your compatriot would act against character when the crucial moment came.

"So what you need is…"

Someone who was a scout and could stand on the front row. Able, as well as respectable. Someone who could keep their business and personal lives separate. Whose alignment was, if not good, at least neutral. And someone who would be likely to take this quest…

"Yes! I can think of one!"

When Guild Girl clapped her hands and jumped out of her seat, Spearman gave her a dubious look. The brief moment that look scanned her chest was not lost on Guild Girl, but at the moment she didn't care.

"Huh? Is there really someone like that?"

"I can guarantee he's skilled, anyway." She went so far as to give him a smile and a wink, then marched off in high spirits. She looked impressive, her shoes clacking as she walked with the paper clutched to her chest. She was headed for the bench in a corner of the Guild waiting area. The place *he* always sat. She found she got a little thrill of happiness just to see the steel helmet turn toward her when he noticed her coming.

And then he asked, in a low, dispassionate voice:

"...Goblins?"

§

"Gotta say, I never thought you'd accept."

"Because there were no goblin-slaying quests."

Thus the three adventurers found themselves in front of the tower. Spearman and Goblin Slayer, with Heavy Warrior the leader.

A party made of one male human warrior, a second male human warrior, and a third male human warrior. It would bring a dry smile to anyone's face. Although these kinds of parties were not uncommon, through sheer necessity.

"And I needed money."

"Mostly for goblin slaying, I assume?" Spearman chuckled.

But Goblin Slayer replied, "No," and shook his head. "Not for that. But it's urgent."

"Depending how much you need, I could loan you some," Heavy Warrior said, never taking his eyes off the tower in front of them. "I figure you wouldn't die on me."

"I appreciate it, but no, thank you."

"Your call." Heavy Warrior responded with a nod, and Goblin Slayer began to dig in his item pouch. The first thing his rummaging produced was a bundle of pitons and a small mallet.

"And I already have a debt to repay."

"Debt? Whatever!" Spearman frowned and gave an annoyed click of his tongue. "We're adventurers! We finish this quest, consider that debt erased."

"I see."

"Anyway, you literally only treated me to a single drink after that. You still owe me!"

"That's the opposite of what you just said," Heavy Warrior said with exasperation, only half-listening to the two of them.

Goblin Slayer brought out a coil of rope and put it around his shoulder.

"I promised to treat you to a drink. And I did."

"Hrrrgh!" Spearman had no reply to Goblin Slayer's pointed comeback. Heavy Warrior had to struggle to hold back a smile.

Angrily muttering, "Hrmph, hrmph," and clicking his tongue, Spearman gave the wall a couple of experimental taps. "…A-anyway, this wall looks awfully solid. Sure you'll be able to set your climbing equipment in it?"

There was some sleight of hand at work, but the other two were not going to be drawn in, either. The tower had been created in a night or two. It was obviously not made of normal materials.

"Here, let me have those."

"Sure." Goblin Slayer passed the pitons and mallet to the outstretched hand.

Heavy Warrior took them, giving one of the anchors a good smack with the mallet, then he groaned.

"Yeah. That's pretty tough."

The gleaming tower wall was not even scratched.

Suddenly, Heavy Warrior began removing his gloves and bracers. He shoved the equipment into his backpack and traded it for a bottle filled with a red liquid. He pulled out the stopper and gulped it down. Probably a strength potion. He put away the empty bottle, then took out a single-handed sword and a ring with a shining ruby.

"Huh! A ring with a physical-boost enchantment?" Spearman said with interest.

It wasn't surprising that Heavy Warrior had a magical sword. Magical weapons were rare, but a Silver rank could be expected to have at least one of them.

"Normally I use my Bracers of Exceptional Swordsmanship and my magic gloves, so I don't need this too often." Heavy Warrior put the sword at his waist and held the piton in the hand with the ring on it. This time he grunted, "Hmph!" and drove it easily into the wall.

"Have a look, Goblin Slayer. That is first-class adventuring equipment for you."

Why are you the one bragging? Heavy Warrior seemed to want to ask.

Spearman ignored him. "Why don't you keep an enchanted sword or two around? Don't you want to look cool?"

"I have no interest in magical swords, but I do have a ring."

"Oh yeah?"

"It allows underwater breathing," Goblin Slayer said briefly. "Even if the goblins stole it, it would do no harm."

"What would they even want it for? Wait a second—you just *assume* it'll get stolen?"

Spearman was pressing on his temples, but the steel helmet nodded and said, "Of course. It wouldn't fit on a goblin finger."

"You oughtta learn it doesn't matter what you say to that guy—it's all useless." Heavy Warrior was fighting back a smile as he grabbed the piton and pulled himself up. "Hey, you both pay me for the potion, right? We split the reward three ways, minus the cost."

And then, holding himself in place with just one arm, he took out another piton and continued climbing. He wasn't exactly zipping along, but he looked pretty good. He was, after all, in full armor and carrying a broadsword across his back. It required no mean physical strength.

"No problem."

"Yeah, sure."

Goblin Slayer responded with alacrity, and Spearman voiced no particular objection. Most adventurers knew to keep any disputes about the reward in the tavern. It didn't matter how valuable an item was, if you kept it at the cost of your life.

Goblin Slayer grabbed the pitons and started up after Heavy Warrior, while behind him Spearman gave a click of his tongue. "So I'm the caboose, huh?"

Goblin Slayer stopped in midclimb, glancing back with one hand still on the piton.

"Would you rather go ahead of me?"

"Tank first, scout second. All good, so come on, keep climbing."

"I see."

He grabbed on, pulled himself up, grabbed the next piton, put his foot on the previous one, and then he was another level higher. What remained was simply to repeat the process. Not looking up, not looking down. Watching cautiously only to the left and right.

All of them were relatively experienced adventurers, and they had handholds and footholds. If they had been so much as worried about the wind, which grew stronger the farther up they went, they couldn't have contemplated climbing the outer wall.

The problem was, the wind wasn't the only thing that could hurt them.

Goblin Slayer, checking left and right as their scout, called out, "Hey." He went on, "To the west. Three of them. Winged. Not goblins."

"So they found us… What color are they?"

"Gray."

"I knew it," Heavy Warrior said, nodding at the answer. "Those'll be gargoyles, no question."

"Gargoyles… Hmm," Goblin Slayer breathed. "So that's what they look like."

"There's a chance they're stone demons. But eighty or ninety percent, yeah."

They were winged demons as dark as the ash in the corner of a fireplace.

Or so one might think at a glance. Such were the stone monsters, gargoyles. Once intended to watch over sacred places, gargoyles, too, were now Non-Prayers. Perhaps it was their terrible, twisted bodies that had, over the course of years, driven them to Chaos.

One wouldn't think that a little bit of flapping could keep a statue in the air, but these creatures could fly. Yet they were made of stone, making them fearsome enemies.

"You've really never seen one? They show up in ruins sometimes."

"A few times." Goblin Slayer slowly turned his head from one side to the other. "But I didn't know they were gargoyles."

"Whatever, they go down quick." Spearman's smile was as fierce as a shark's. The monsters now flew—literally—into his field of view.

They had been making lazy corkscrews around the top of the tower, probably keeping watch. Now they came down in a panic—chances were they hadn't expected anyone to try climbing the wall. They weren't far away, but the adventurers didn't seem very frightened or show any sign of becoming so.

"It ain't true what they say, that gargoyles can't stand sunlight." Spearman glared up at them, adjusting his feet to find his balance on the pitons. "If they get ahold of you, you're in for a fight."

Holding himself steady with his shielded left arm, Goblin Slayer drew his sword in a reverse grip. "If you can get it under you, you won't die even if you fall to the ground. Although you would be away from the battle at that point."

"Maybe, if you could cast Control on 'em. And that's if they don't go down in one hit, right?" Heavy Warrior pulled out his one-handed sword, which gave off a faint white glow—the aura of magic. He held the decorative string that hung from the hilt in his mouth, then fastened it securely around his wrist. "I don't know about you, but I'm fine with just one hand."

"They say the clash of spells comes before the clash of arms. Arrgh. These muscle-brains." Spearman narrowed his eyes and touched his earring—a magical catalyst—with one hand. Goblin Slayer glanced down at what Spearman was doing, then shook his head.

"I am thinking of something."

"Me, too," said Heavy Warrior.

"Shut up, I get it! I can't concentrate down here!"

"GARGLEGARGLEGARGLE!!"

With an indistinct bellow not unlike gargling, the demon-like monsters came flying at them. But Spearman, without hurry or fuss, spoke a few words of true power with the ability to reshape the very laws of reality.

"*Hora...semel...silento!* Stand silent, time!"

That instant, the wind stopped.

The flow of the atmosphere ceased; the sound from afar paused, stagnated, halted. Spearman's words filled the world, bending its laws, and everything stalled.

This was the spell Slow.

"GARGLEGARG?! GARGLEGARG!!"

"GARGLEGARGLEGAR!!"

The gargoyles flapped and flapped but could generate no power, so they could not stay in the air. Gravity took hold of the three creatures, and in a matter of seconds they had fallen several dozen stories, shattering back to dust as they hit the ground. And no stone statue, once destroyed, could return to life again.

"What, all gone? They weren't so tough."

"I suppose a fall from this height does generally lead to death."

Heavy Warrior pursed his lips, disappointed, and Goblin Slayer slid his sword back into its scabbard. The two of them quickly resumed climbing, but Spearman shot them an unmistakably discontented look.

"Geez, a spell like that, and you can't even muster one word of praise?"

"It was a good strategy," came back Goblin Slayer's casual response. "I will use it sometime."

"What, on goblins?"

"What else?"

This exchange caused Spearman to shake his head with a heartfelt weariness. Take goblins up high somewhere and then drop them? It didn't sound like something most serious adventurers would contemplate. And to think he was being credited with the idea—*Gimme a break!*

"More important: how many spells do you have left?" Heavy Warrior's words brought Spearman back to himself.

He grabbed a piton to steady himself, nearly too late, and called up, "One more." It pained him to admit it, but a fact was a fact. "This isn't my main class, remember."

"All right, if we're attacked on the climb again, we head back down and rest for a night. Then we'll switch to a head-on assault."

Heavy Warrior's decision was swift and sure. To attack the enemy base with their spells exhausted or after they had been restored? No matter how you looked at it, the latter offered a better chance of survival.

Spearman understood that, and he grinned. "Even if we're about to touch the sky?"

"If we're right there, then it's different," Heavy Warrior replied, flashing his teeth as he laughed at Spearman's lighthearted jab.

"You're the leader." Goblin Slayer nodded quietly. "I will follow your orders."

"Good. In that case, on we go." Heavy Warrior held out a hand for more pitons; Goblin Slayer dug in his pouch and brought out another bundle. He kept plenty with him because they were such a useful tool, and thanks to that there seemed likely to be no question of them having enough to reach the summit.

"Anyway, I guess they know we're here. Let's make sure they roll out the red carpet."

"Right."

Goblin Slayer made his short response and looked up at the man ahead of him. The vast broadsword across Heavy Warrior's back was quivering with a rattle. In an immensely serious, grave tone, Goblin Slayer said, "Don't drop that on me."

"Aw, shaddup."

Spearman guffawed without any malice, and Heavy Warrior sullenly continued to exert his muscles.

Their objective, the top of the tower, was not far away.

§

The spire's summit presented an almost indescribable scene.

It was an open space with a depression like a round bowl, the outside ringed with pillars. The roof was a curved dome, as if a massive globe were descending into the space. On the ceiling was a star map, but its wild lines reflected no constellations any of the adventurers knew about.

The floor and the pillars were pure white, the blue sky peeking between the colonnades. And yet, there was a crushing sense of oppression. As Heavy Warrior drew himself up over the edge, he looked at the constellations and gave an unhappy wheeze.

"This is Chaos work for sure. Let's go, and let's not leave anything to cause us trouble later."

He reached out a hand as he spoke, taking hold of a leather glove. He helped Goblin Slayer up, and the latter took in the surroundings.

"The climb was easier than I expected."

"Probably because we're three guys." Heavy Warrior pulled the ring off his finger and put it back in his item bag. He quickly replaced it with his gloves and bracers, grabbing the broadsword from his back. "Wouldn't want some kids to have to make that climb."

"Man, that's for sure." The reply came from Spearman, who hesitated, frowning at the leather glove hovering in front of him. The plain, unsophisticated mitt took Spearman's hand, pulling the last member of the party onto the roof. "I'd hate to make *her* do this. Heck, she probably couldn't. A bit too top-heavy."

The uncouth remark sounded strangely inoffensive coming from Spearman, though that was perhaps thanks to his personality. Heavy Warrior shot him a dubious look as he made a broad gesture in front of his chest with both hands.

"I do understand what you're saying," Goblin Slayer said, with another reserved nod. "One would not wish to tire out one's back row. And mine is sensitive."

"Is *that* what you're worried about?" Spearman sighed deeply. "Don't you have anything else? Women's bodies are supposed to be praised! Busts! Hips! Butts!"

"What is the point of praising them?"

"They love you for it, and you get to be popular with the ladies!"

"I see."

Goblin Slayer failed to rise to the bait any further, instead drawing his sword. He checked the strap of his shield, then rotated his right wrist, along with the weapon in its grip. Heavy Warrior glanced at him.

"Didn't use up too much strength?"

"I'm fine."

"Good." Heavy Warrior slapped Goblin Slayer gently on the shoulder. "What about you?"

"I'm not as fragile as all that," Spearman grinned, taking his spear in both hands and giving it a playful thrust.

For the leader to show that he understood how each member of the party was doing was an important way of relieving any anxiety on the part of the group.

And all the more so before a climactic battle. Heavy Warrior kept the point of his broadsword trained on a single spot on the rooftop. He ran his tongue over his lips to wet them.

"Let's get started."

And then, the enemy was there.

A swirling shadow in the middle of the roof, at the bottom of the bowl-shaped depression. Darkness gathered toward the wriggling, rising shadow. At length, it formed an old-fashioned overcoat, the figure wavering like a mirage.

"Foolish mortals…!"

The voice creaked like a dry branch, a sound a human most likely couldn't make.

The figure was wasted and bent and looked as if it were standing in a swamp. In its knobbed fingers, it clasped a staff that appeared as old as its hands. Below its coat, a spirit flame burned. The man, the indisputable image of an evil wizard, spat at the hateful adventurers:

"How I loathe any who would interfere with my pl—!"

But he was cut off before he could finish.

A sword.

A crude, mass-produced sword of a strange length sliced through the air, its aim true, and pierced the wizard's chest. He let out a gurgle, then fell to the ground, clawing at his throat.

"Hey, hey, you could at least let him finish. Is this it?"

"There is no need for us to confront him head-on."

It was Goblin Slayer. Standing next to the smirking Spearman, the man who had launched his sword through the air shook his steel helmet from side to side. "And it appears he was not a serious opponent."

Indeed.

The wizard had collapsed with a thump. As they watched, the sword in his chest withered away. It turned to rust before they could blink. A bony hand reached up, grasped and shattered it.

"The ritual…is already…complete!" he howled as he pulled out the decimated blade. It was abundantly clear that this person was a Non-Prayer Character.

Heavy Warrior stood with his broadsword at the ready and glanced at Goblin Slayer.

"Maybe stabbing him in the chest wasn't the best plan?"

"It's about the height of a goblin's head."

Goblin Slayer had pulled out a dagger and settled into a low stance.

Spirit fire flickered in the wizard's eyes as he shuffled forward.

"I cannot be killed by those who have words…!"

"You heard him," Spearman said, almost as if stifling a yawn. "What do we do?"

"He said he cannot be killed, but he didn't say he cannot die."

Heavy Warrior grinned like he had when he'd bested his first giant roach. He nodded the way Goblin Slayer did when faced with a goblin.

"Only one thing to do, then."

Without so much as a nod to each other, the party fell into formation and prepared for battle.

The wizard began shouting true words without a moment's hesitation, bending space. With two or three words he invoked a spell, and what appeared—perhaps to be expected—were gray stone demons. They waited faithfully behind their master, and then, at a sweep of his staff, they launched themselves at the adventurers.

"Boorish barbarians! Yield before my vast intelligence!"

But the men against him were all warriors and had all achieved Silver rank. The hard work and perseverance that had led to Heavy Warrior's skill with the sword were nothing to sneeze at.

"You forgot 'great'!"

Heavy Warrior groaned as he plunged forward to meet the monsters and hold them to the left, right, and center.

"GARGLEGARGLEGA!!"

"GARGLE!! GARGLEGA!!"

When a careless statue came within reach, he seized the opportunity and destroyed it.

He struck an intimidating pose. This was a man who needed nothing but a sword and his own body. It would take more than numbers to faze him. With each sweep of his sword, dust trailed through the air like a banner.

"Then die like the barbarians you are!" the wizard cried, still wielding his staff from safely behind his gargoyles.

"*Tonitrus…oriens…!* Rise, thunder!"

Summoned by the words of true power, magic began welling up in the area. There was no wind, yet the adventurers were hit by an overwhelming force like an oncoming storm.

"'Lightning'?!" Spearman shouted. He saw what was happening and stayed alert for his chance. "I could use Counterspell… No, it'd never work! I'm sorry, guys, I can't do it!"

But this came in part from the recognition that his opponent was a far more accomplished magic user than he.

"Okay," Heavy Warrior nodded, dispensing orders at a breakneck pace as he slaughtered yet another gargoyle. "Cover your mouths!"

"Cover your mouths," Goblin Slayer repeated. His dagger was no longer in his hand; he was already searching through his item pouch.

He pulled out the egg and threw it in a single motion. Heavy Warrior pulled up the collar of his coat.

The egg described a beautiful parabola, but the wizard swatted it down like a fly and stepped on it.

"Very clever, you——?!"

Instantaneously, a red mist floated up from his feet—powder and bits of shell. A paralyzing pain struck his mouth and nose and eyes. He couldn't breathe or speak. Or, of course, chant magic. The wizard pressed his hands to his face and fell back with a voiceless scream.

The powder was a tear gas, including capsicum and other ingredients. However advanced one might be in magic, so long as one had eyes and nose and mouth, it was difficult to avoid.

"Now…you're…mine!"

Spearman lost no time; he shot across the floor like an arrow from a bow. The gargoyles, pinned down by Heavy Warrior, were nothing to him. He headed straight for the wizard, touching a hand to his earring.

"*Aranea…facio…ligator!* Spider, come and bind!"

"?!"

The "spider web" easily caught up the agonized wizard. The wizard's spirit flame guttered—and the instant it did so, the tip of a spear drove through his heart.

The blood that sprayed out was bluish-black. Spearman quickly gave the silk-wrapped body a kick to free his weapon and jumped back.

Needless to say, as he had declared earlier, the wizard showed no sign of losing his life to this. With gobs of blue-black blood pouring from his mouth, he tried to open his lips wide enough to speak another spell…

"Aw, shut it."

Spearman wound the end of the spider web on the tip of his spear and used it as a gag. He shrugged at the wizard, who seemed unwilling to give up, his spirit flame burning with murderous intent.

"Looks like you weren't kidding when you said you couldn't be killed."

"You don't have to worry about a wizard who can't speak," Heavy Warrior said. "But it is a bit of a pain," he muttered as he smashed the last of the gargoyles with his broadsword.

All that remained was to find the source of the wizard's power, which had to be somewhere in the tower, and destroy it.

But so long as the sorcerer was alive, it was likely the traps and monsters would not disappear.

"Hmm," Heavy Warrior grunted. Beside him, Goblin Slayer kept his dagger trained on their captive, ever vigilant. Then his helmet tilted somewhat, as if he had just thought of something.

"Why not just drop him?"

"…"

"…"

Heavy Warrior and Spearman shared a glance. They nodded and then laughed like naughty children.

"That's it."

"Let's do it."

The wizard, trying to speak around the gag in his mouth, was dragged to the edge of the tower and then given a firm kick in the back. Gravity had no words, yet it dragged him down, and soon he had met the same fate as the earlier adventurers.

In other words, he died easily.

"I wonder why he built this tower, anyway," Spearman commented aloud, peering over the side at the bluish-black stain spreading on the ground below. His type usually set up shop either at the tip-top of a tower or in the lowest reaches of an underground maze. "It might have been more trouble to kill him if he'd been way underground."

"Maybe he had a handout from the gods or something," Heavy

Warrior said bluntly, returning his broadsword to his back. He was still watching their surroundings carefully, perhaps because the danger of traps and remaining enemies had not lessened. "Come on, let's find the loot. The boss is dead. If we don't hurry, this tower might vanish."

"Oh yeah, that's right! An adventure's gotta have treasure!"

Spearman set off running, his joy giving him courage. Heavy Warrior did not even consider stopping him. Attitude and actions were separate. Just as keeping your guard up and not being nervous were different things.

"He's pretty good that way."

"Yes." Goblin Slayer nodded, picking up the rust-ruined sword and clicking his tongue as he tossed it away. "There are many things I could learn from him."

"I can't tell if you're joking or not."

While Heavy Warrior considered whether to laugh, he and Goblin Slayer set out on the search. They were looking for loot, treasure chests, effects—anything of the sort. For an adventurer, there was no greater joy.

In short order, they discovered a storage chest of red oak sitting in a corner of the roof.

"This is not my main class. Don't expect too much," Goblin Slayer warned them, then knelt before the chest. He rooted through his item pack and produced several specialized tools. First, he took a file like a thin blade and worked it under the lid of the chest, feeling around. He confirmed there were no traps, then held up a hand mirror to the keyhole and looked in.

Now it was time for the wire. Goblin Slayer set to picking the lock.

"Hey, Goblin Slayer. Think about this: you didn't stop a single bad guy today." Spearman grinned as he watched the work over Goblin Slayer's shoulder. "Meaning..."

"What?"

"I win!"

"Yes," Goblin Slayer made no effort to refute him, only nodded. "So you do."

Spearman flung his fist into the air with many a celebratory "Yesss!" Heavy Warrior stared up at the sky.

"Because it was not goblins."

In his elation, Spearman seemed to miss the murmur, but Heavy Warrior certainly heard it.

At last, the lock opened with a click, and Goblin Slayer exhaled.

"It is a bit late to mention this, but there will probably be some fuss when we return."

"Huh? ...Oh, your elf girl?" Heavy Warrior thought of the tomboyish, excitable elf in Goblin Slayer's party.

I guess we did kind of leave her out.

"I think I'm gonna be in even more trouble," Spearman said. "But don't worry. It's tradition to have little excitement while you divide the spoils and drink some wine."

"...As I recall, we said it would be three ways less expenses."

"Yes," Goblin Slayer said, "I believe so." Then he added in a dispassionate voice, "Treasure, huh? Not bad."

Heavy Warrior placed a friendly hand on his shoulder. Goblin Slayer accepted it silently. The lid of the chest squeaked as he lifted it.

CHAPTER 7

Of the Second Time the Necromancer's Plans Were Upset

"Fwaaaah!"

As the hero awoke with the morning sun, in a bed at the inn, she stretched her arms mightily. The sky outside was blue, and she felt energetic, strong, and ready to go.

"Okay! Today's another day to give it everything I've got!"

She energized herself with a quick slap to each cheek, then used that energy to spring out of bed.

This was important, because the warm sunlight was so comfortable it made her want to climb right back under the covers. But it would be just a little bit too indulgent to squander such a beautiful day on oversleeping.

She quickly dressed. Her body was still youthful, but it had the curves of a maturing woman. Thinking about what was to come later that day, she made sure to wear her armor, too. Finally, she took up her enchanted sword, her faithful companion, and she was ready. One had to equip oneself with both weapons and armor, or there was no point.

"Gooood morning, everybody!"

She flung open the door and leaped into the hallway, going nimbly from the atrium to the first floor.

Luckily, due to the early hour, there were not many people in the tavern yet. The only one watching her as she made her silent landing was a wide-eyed waitress on a morning shift.

Sword Master—her companion, who had already gotten up and eaten an early breakfast—gave a sigh of scant surprise. "…Look at you, all bright-eyed and bushy-tailed after a night's sleep. What are you, a kid?"

"Huh? Isn't this normal?" Hero plopped down across from Sword Master with her head cocked, letting her legs dangle. She immediately grabbed some bread from the basket in the middle of the table, slathering it with butter and stuffing it into her mouth.

Mmm, delicious!

"Oh, I'll have… Let's see. I want the sausage and fried egg!"

"Y-yes, ma'am! Right away!"

"Oh, and bread! With plenty of butter!"

The waitress observed this audacious behavior in a daze, then scuttled off to the kitchen.

"Huh? Is our third still asleep?"

"Things did go late last night."

Sword Master smacked Hero's hand, which was outstretched for another piece of bread, and looked up at the bedrooms on the second floor. He appeared concerned about Sage, who was not yet awake.

"Well, there were an awful lot of them!"

"And our party is not able to use Dispel."

That meant they could not return ghosts and undead to the earth. As a result, they had to cut off the head of the Necromancer's army—literally. If the king had not taken the bulk of the enemy forces, it would have been very difficult.

"It would be so great if I could just clear all the way to the horizon with one sweep!"

"Stop that. If you could do that, it would be terrifically dangerous."

"You think?"

As she mumbled, "Really…?" and swung her legs, Hero very much gave the impression of a little girl. Sword Master found it hard to believe she was *the* hero—in the best way. All he could do was swing a sword, but he wanted to help her if he could.

"Oh, hey, I had a weird dream."

"A dream?"

"Yeah. The gods, right? They were like, *Go to that one town.*"

Sword Master took pause when she said this. He had no knowledge of such magic or divine secrets. His understanding extended to "kill this, stab that."

"...That is an Oracle, a handout."

The subdued voice came from above.

A girl wearing an overcoat and holding a staff came trotting down the stairs, rubbing her eyes. Sage—one of the great spell casters of this world.

"Morning!" Hero waved at her, and Sage replied with a nod. She pulled out a chair and sat down. Hero narrowed her eyes in happiness at the familiar sight of the three of them around a table.

"...What kind of town?"

"Hmm. Maybe they were having a festival? There was this...kind of fuzzy light."

"Is that everything?"

"And there was this huge storm, like *bwah!* Maybe it was a giant?"

"...I have a guess."

Sage murmured one or two words to create a spell and pulled a rounded sheepskin paper out of thin air. Sword Master had no idea what was going on, but she occasionally produced things this way. Spread on the table, it turned out to be a map of the frontier. Sage pointed to a certain spot with the end of her staff.

"...Here."

"All riiiight!"

Hero made a fist just as the waitress arrived with her food, saying, "Sorry for the wait."

"Want anything?" Sword Master asked, and Sage replied briefly, "An omelet."

Hero laughed as she applied ketchup liberally to her fried egg.

"I guess we know where our next adventure will be!"

It was true: adventures took place everywhere in this world.

CHAPTER 8

Of an Elf's Lazy Day

"Hrrm…?"

The sun was well into the sky when its rays came through the window and struck the eyes of High Elf Archer. She was naked, curled up in bed under a single blanket, and she buried her face in the pillow in a short-lived show of resistance. But the sunlight was fearsomely bright. It could not be defeated simply by covering her face.

Soon giving in, the elf yawned like a cat—*fwaah*—and gave a great stretch of her lean body.

"Faah…oooh… 'S it morning?"

The sun was a bit too high for morning. It was nearly noon.

High Elf Archer, rubbing her eyes and looking out the window, sat up cross-legged in bed.

"Ooo…"

She clawed at her sleep-addled hair as she mumbled meaningless syllables.

As she recalled, she had today off. At least, if no one came to wake her, it meant there was no adventure.

That Orcbolg—he had gone off alone, all *goblins, goblins* as usual.

She honestly wasn't sure about the recent incident. She had trouble believing a battle with an evil wizard on top of a tower.

In any case, this sure is different from the forest.

If nothing else, the fact that she could sleep until noon made her glad she had left the woods.

She yawned again, then scratched at her healthily taut belly and belly button. High-elf behavior was known for its refinement, but there were limits.

High Elf Archer stretched out her legs toward the floor, which was so cluttered with items and possessions that there was barely anywhere to put her feet. The tips of her toes found her beloved great bow. She retied the loosened string, then plucked it gently to check it. She ought to change it sooner or later.

"Hmm, I'm sure it was around… Ah, there you are."

She sprawled on her bed and stretched her arms out toward the floor.

She picked up a little spider about the size of a fingertip. It had been wandering around on top of her leggings on the ground.

High Elf Archer tapped a slim finger on the spider's behind and gave a tug, and a silver thread ran into the air. She was literally spinning silk. And not sticky web silk, but the plain kind spiders used to walk on. She did this two or three times, until she had the lengths of thread she wanted, whereupon her ears quivered.

"That's enough, I guess. Thanks!"

She let the spider go and set about twisting the thread. Spider's silk was light but stronger than steel wire of the same thickness. The perfect material for a bowstring. After a while, the elf had wound the strings together. She ran them back and forth through her fingers, from one end to the other.

Convinced there were no problems, she flitted her ears in satisfaction.

"There we go."

She wound the string into a loop and popped out of bed and onto the floor. Being careful not to step on borrowed books and toys she had bought but didn't really understand, she worked her way around the room.

She swept up her hunter's garb, slipping it on carelessly.

Today was her day off. She didn't need her overcoat or anything. Although a short sword might be appropriate…

She was slim and elegant; she had skin so white it was almost translucent and not a lot of extra meat on her bones. Combined with her flat chest, she had the beauty of a carved statue.

In beauty, at least, forest elves were not content to come second to any other race. Perhaps the reason they hid themselves under clothing was that they saw their own fairness as simply normal.

"~♪"

Whistling tunelessly, High Elf Archer braided her hair. She gently brushed aside the stray strands from her shoulders and cheeks, and when she spun back around, her messy room greeted her.

In some ways, the mayhem was understandable in the room of an adventurer. But it was hard to believe this was the room of a young woman, and an elf at that. Equipment had been tossed around, discarded clothing lay everywhere, and empty dishes were piled up carelessly. Adventure novels and books of plays lay open, while playthings bought at temple festivals were scattered about. It would be easier to believe this was a child's bedroom.

How did so many things even fit in such a relatively small space? It was a great riddle that even the elves, with all their knowledge, could not have fathomed.

"Hmm," High Elf Archer crossed her arms gravely and surveyed the room, then batted her long ears and nodded as if in agreement with something. "I'd better do some laundry."

§

She added shaved soap and her clothes to a tub full of water from the well, then put in her bare feet.

"Oooh… Underground water is cold, isn't it?"

Her body and ears both shuddered, and she began treading on her clothing.

She knew for certain: she could never have imagined this back in her forest home. There, it had been a simple matter of putting your clothes in the river and asking the undines or other water spirits to wash them for you. Household chores were left to brownies. The human world was awfully inconvenient, she thought.

But all that aside, she did enjoy stomping around, basically playing in the water.

Behind the Guild was a watering hole that also served as a place to do the wash.

The warm light of the late morning sun poured down. In the distance, she could hear children running and housewives chatting. Lunch preparations must have been under way, because a tempting aroma drifted from the tavern kitchen.

High Elf Archer loved this time. Somehow it had a different smell from the usual town mornings and nights and days when she was going on an adventure. She didn't know exactly what that smell was, and she might have been imagining it. She found a healthy curiosity well and good in both herself and others, but some things ought to go without being too thoroughly investigated.

"Bwaaah…"

She gave another wide yawn. No matter how much you slept, on days like this it was never enough. But then, elves had all the time in the world. Wasting a little of it wouldn't hurt anything.

It is kind of a shame, though.

Interesting things, things that got her attention—if she took her eyes off them for just a moment, suddenly they would be gone.

High Elf Archer continued stamping on the laundry, giving another great yawn and stepping out of the bucket. Then she squeezed out her well-trod clothes and spread them out left and right with a *whap.*

"Lots of interesting things to think about, really."

Like the delicate scent of soap. The breeze she could feel through her damp clothing. The sunlight.

Enjoying all these things, High Elf Archer hung her clothes from the line in the wash area. She remembered all too well when she had hung them carelessly and they had gotten wrinkled, so she made sure to make them as neat as possible. For some reason, it was troubling when they got caught by the wind and blown onto the ground, so she fastened them securely with clothespins.

"Done and done!"

She hung the last garment carefully, then gave a satisfied flick of her ears. She wiped her forehead, although it wasn't sweaty, put her hands on her hips, and eyed the laundry. The clothing flapped in the wind like the banner of an army atop a conquered fortress.

"Doing the laundry? Aren't you a hard worker."

High Elf Archer turned toward the voice behind her with a proud sniff.

In general, elves could tell who was coming without looking. But even they could be surprised sometimes. There are exceptions to every rule.

"Oh, Guild Girl. What's up?"

"I have the day off, so I'm just wandering."

The receptionist was wearing personal clothes. It was a bit of a shock, because High Elf Archer was so used to seeing her in her uniform, but of course, even Guild Girl owned other outfits. Just like everyone.

She was wearing a light summer dress. It had no sleeves, showing the lovely line of her arms from her shoulders to her neatly trimmed nails. It sat easily on her and would probably let a cooling breeze through nicely. Her well-formed body was presumably a result of the effort she put in every day. It could comfortably be called ideal.

"It makes you look like a sylph, somehow."

Guild Girl smiled, pleased at this. "I got it because it's supposed to be the latest fashion in the Capital."

So that was it. High Elf Archer nodded. It certainly seemed like a good outfit to just wander in. Human fashion, though, changed at such a frenzied pace that she found it difficult to keep up with…

I wonder how they come up with so many things in a single year.

One thing was certain: the human world never got boring.

"But why are you at the Guild?"

It was her day off. Guild Girl averted her eyes suddenly at High Elf Archer's innocent question. Her gaze shifted from one place to another.

"…Just because. I thought maybe I'd make sure our adventurers had come home all right."

"Huh!" High Elf Archer laughed, not reflecting particularly deeply on this answer. "Now that's dedication!"

"Well, you know…" Guild Girl said evasively. "So how goes your washing?"

"Behold, the fruits of my labor." High Elf Archer stuck out her little chest proudly. "What do you think?"

It wasn't like she had used a special skill. It was just laundry. Not something to brag about, but Guild Girl smiled anyway.

"You've gotten pretty used to doing it, haven't you?" she commented.

"I guess so. I can handle this much pretty easily," replied High Elf Archer.

"Oh… No underwear?"

"?"

Guild Girl stood with her braids bobbing as she tilted her head quizzically.

High Elf Archer answered readily, "I don't have any."

"Oh, you mean this is your second wash already?"

"No," she replied with an emphatic shake of her head. *Why didn't she understand?* "I don't *have* any."

"…I thought we all picked some out together a while ago."

"I kinda buried it…"

"…"

Guild Girl was pressing on her brow and staring at the ground just long enough for High Elf Archer to be slightly suspicious. And when Guild Girl looked up again…

"Let's go buy some, then. Yes, let's do that."

There was that pasted-on smile.

"Huh? But… Honestly, they're kind of a pain…"

"Let's go."

And for an adventurer to refuse an offer from a Guild employee was simply not possible.

§

"Errgh… Hey, do I really have to put this on?"

"Yes, you do!"

High Elf Archer peeked out of the changing room to find Guild Girl's finger stuck in her face.

Guild Girl had taken the elf by the scruff of the neck and dragged her to the town's general store.

This may have been an underdeveloped area of the frontier, but even here there was a tailor.

"Although, when it comes to the latest things from the Capital, you'll have better luck at the general store."

It might not hold a candle to the water town, but more items came through here.

So Guild Girl had said and stuck out her well-formed chest, but High Elf Archer didn't understand. Fashion changed with such blinding speed, maybe only humans could keep up.

"And what's more," Guild Girl said with a shake of her finger, "appearance is important to adventurers."

"It is?"

"If higher-ranked adventurers don't look the part, it drags down the overall quality of all our adventurers."

Adventurers were known for a particular appearance, all right: ruffians with weapons and armor. The state may have established the Guild to help manage adventurers, but public opinion was not so generous. There was no need for outrageous clothing, but a well-tended appearance was important.

It wasn't that High Elf Archer didn't understand that logic. She did understand it, and yet…

"Yeah?" she said with a displeased wave of her ears. "Try telling *him* that."

"You think he'd listen?" Guild Girl shot back with a broad smile.

"…No," High Elf Archer said, sulking back into the changing room. In her hand she held thin and sleeveless lingerie that came down to her midriff.

"But I've got high hopes for you, you know."

"High hopes?"

"Elves naturally have such beautiful skin—you probably don't even need to groom yourself."

"I don't know about that…"

Nonetheless, High Elf Archer gave a dismissive grunt and squeezed herself into the underwear. She just couldn't get used to the sensation of it stuck to her flat chest.

"I promised to help our little friend pick out some underwear, too."

Just for a second, Guild Girl seemed to offer a peek behind her stiff smile. "We're all girls, right? You may be adventurers, and equipment might be more important than fashion, but..." High Elf Archer's ears picked up the last few words as she murmured, "But we're all girls, right?"

There was nothing critical or scolding in her tone. Maybe she wasn't in a position to do such a thing. High Elf Archer didn't know. But even if she didn't understand it, she could tell Guild Girl was caring for them in her own way.

She is a good person. I think.

"But still..."

Be that as it may. Underwear might help in absorbing sweat and such, but...

She had grabbed a single piece of thin clothing, an upside-down triangle. The color on top and bottom, of course, matched.

...I don't think this thing could even do that much.

She held up the thing in her hand, stretching it and scrutinizing it as she said, "Why would you wear this?"

"What do you mean, why?"

"I mean, it's not like anyone's going to see it. Who would you show it to?"

She could sense Guild Girl stiffening on the far side of the changing room curtain.

"Hm?" High Elf Archer said, surprised, with a tilt of her head. Apparently she had asked something else she wasn't supposed to.

"It-it's kind of in preparation for...for when the time comes to show it to someone. Underwear is a girl's last trump card," Guild Girl said while remaining as gentle as ever.

"Is that right?" High Elf Archer asked offhandedly, to which Guild Girl said bluntly, "Yes, it is."

Hmm...

It was hard for her to imagine that such a slim, unreliable-looking piece of clothing could be all that.

Maybe Guild Girl could sense High Elf Archer mulling this over, because she muttered, "Oh, well. You don't have to force yourself to buy it right now or anything, but you should think about it."

"Sure, I will."

High Elf Archer tore off the clothes she'd been trying on without a moment's regret. Then she grabbed up her own garments, which had been scattered on the floor, and squeezed into them as fast as she could. From the other side of the curtain, she could hear Guild Girl exclaim, "Y-yikes!" as the lingerie came flying over.

"If you put on clothes over these and then tried to move, it seems like they would be kind of...fluffy and rustly." High Elf Archer bounded out of the changing room, back in her usual garb, and looked Guild Girl in the eye. She was picking up the clothes the elf had flung to the ground. High Elf Archer smiled without malice, like a cat. "I'd rather do something fun. Hey, wanna play a game?"

§

"A tabletop game?"

"Right. I just found it recently."

Thus they came to the Guild tavern some time after noon.

Padfoot Waitress gave them a little bow, and High Elf Archer took the chairs off one of the tables.

Guild Girl produced a long, flat box wrapped in a copper-colored cloth. She opened a window and blew some dust off it. On the lid was a winding snake pattern.

"You move pawns, roll dice, and act like an adventurer... At least, I think that's how it works."

"So...you pretend to be an adventurer?"

"More or less."

When they opened the lid of the box, they found several old sheepskin books, along with a collection of pawns and dice, tucked neatly inside. High Elf Archer took one of the figurines in hand and scrutinized it. It stood on a circular base: a knight wearing blue plate armor. Perhaps it was made of metal, because it had heft to it. This figure held a banner with an omega symbol on it, brandished a fine steel blade, and was crying out to end Chaos. A paladin, no doubt.

"This is pretty good craftsmanship."

"There are a lot of scenarios, too. From saving the world to, well, slaying goblins."

High Elf Archer giggled at the words *slaying goblins.* Her long ears bobbed happily.

"I bet it would go south fast if we made Orcbolg play it… Hey, can I ask you something?"

"What?"

"What's the point of this?"

Guild Girl was left blinking by the sudden question. High Elf Archer saw her confusion and waved her hands frantically.

"Sorry, don't take that the wrong way. I mean literally."

"Oh, I see… Hmm." Lost in thought, Guild Girl seemed very much the same as usual, despite being out of uniform. "I guess you could use it to determine your roles and actions before going on an actual adventure, to a certain extent."

The disconnect caused High Elf Archer to snicker, and Guild Girl scratched her cheek.

"But I've never done this before," the elf said.

"It takes effort and time, and of course you need enough players. Plus, a lot of people can't read."

"Hmm…"

She added that although the game was available, it was rarely used.

That was understandable to High Elf Archer. She put the paladin carefully back in the box. "I'm sure it wouldn't be enough to guarantee a smooth adventure."

"That's true. It's completely different from reality, that's for sure."

As she spoke, Guild Girl reached into the box again and took a piece. It was a masculine-looking light warrior, wearing leather armor and holding a dagger at the ready. Perhaps a scout.

"But maybe…that's enough." She touched its face gently with a finger, smiling shyly. "You could welcome back adventurers who had saved the world. It's not quite a fantasy, or a dream…" She spoke quietly, almost as if to hide some embarrassment.

I get it. The elf girl waved her long ears gently and smiled. She could understand. Even though she was on the side being welcomed instead of doing the welcoming.

"Hey, teach me how to play," she said, taking the paladin back out of the box.

Yeah. I like her face.

"Just watch me. I'll save all the worlds you like!"

And then High Elf Archer proceeded to fail. Not only did she not defeat the immortal wizard, but she never even arrived at his maze-like mausoleum. Finding the miasma-laden entrance to the tomb was not for half-baked heroes.

Saving the world turned out to be a Herculean task, even when the world was a game board.

§

"Aww, man! That sucked!"

The tavern at evening was boisterous, and nobody listened to High Elf Archer's exclamation. Sometimes adventures went well, and sometimes they didn't. Sometimes the kindest thing you could do was ignore someone.

"I swear something was wrong there! How can a dragon just come flapping out of the sky?!"

"That was what was in the materials, so that's just how it went."

As the elf sprawled across the table and pounded the wood, Guild Girl responded with an awkward smile.

After that, the world had ultimately been destroyed several times. Despite the addition of Inspector, as well as Priestess and Cow Girl, who had shown up at the bar, peace for the world seemed a distant goal.

"'Just how it went'! Not acceptable." The two-thousand-year-old elf pouted like a child.

"You think?"

"Yeah, I think we could have done something more. I'm sure of it," she complained, giving a wave of her cupful of grape wine.

"Maybe so," Guild Girl said with a measured nod, pulling her food away from the wine droplets that splattered on the table. "Part of the interest of tabletop games is to see what people come up with."

And she had to admit that the setup *had* been a little over-the-top.

At those words, High Elf Archer rolled her head on the table to stare up at Guild Girl.

"...Actually, don't you think it's kind of wasteful?"

"Wasteful?"

"Or…indulgent. You guys barely even live a hundred years, right?"

Notwithstanding the occasional necromancer.

High Elf Archer wiggled her ears, tracing a circle in the air with her pointer finger.

"To use that scant time worrying about the future…it seems like a waste."

"You mean we should be in the moment?" Guild Girl asked, her braids slipping down as she tilted her head.

"Yeah," replied High Elf Archer with a laugh. "It's the privilege of mortals to laugh or cry or get angry or fuss about what went on today. To worry about what happens a hundred or two hundred years from now—that's our business."

"I wonder."

"A high elf said it. It must be true!"

High Elf Archer's reply was accompanied by a proud snort as she confidently thrust out her small chest. She was a long way from the image of a noble high elf enjoining a human to be more thoughtful. But the truth was, she herself felt it took all she had to attend to what was right in front of her day by day.

Guild Girl giggled, and a smile came over her face—not her pasted-on smile, but a completely natural one. At the sight of it, High Elf Archer, quite pleased with what she had accomplished, narrowed her eyes like a cat and smiled.

"Well, since we're here… Excuse me!"

"Yes!"

With Guild Girl still smiling, she called over Padfoot Waitress and ordered another bottle of wine. She was no hedonist, but this was special. Why not drink something good?

She opened the cork, enjoying the aromatic alcohol, then poured it generously into Guild Girl's cup and her own. High Elf Archer took her cup, her eyes sparkling like she'd never seen one before, and Guild Girl did the same.

"…Okay. Here's to today's failed adventure."

"A failure I won't forget if I live to be a hundred!"

Cheers! Their glasses clinked with a musical sound.

©Noboru Kannatuki

CHAPTER 9

Of the Three of Them, Some Months Ago

The word *tavern* could mean many things. Not all such places were attached to Adventurers Guilds.

Wander around town and you'd find several, with bulletin boards and lights shining.

They typically had inns attached, and sometimes adventurers just wanted a change of scenery. These were places where adventurers could easily show up, eat and drink as much as they liked, and then set back off into town.

In one such tavern, a minstrel gave a warbling strum of his instrument and began to sing.

How many times do we meet and part?
What matters, proclaimed you, is what's in the heart
With no one to fancy, they come and they go
Till you saw that sweet thing one day—oh-ho!
Be you a lord or be you a spy,
You don't know her name, but you cherish her eyes
You ply your sweet talk, yet past tavern door
You realize too late: she's not there anymore
How many times do we meet and part?
One meeting, one parting, and one broken heart…

* * *

"A'right, then. Guess we've got ourselves a party, hey, Scaly?"

"Ha-ha-ha. Though I could wish for a warrior and a scout."

Sitting well inside the cozy tavern, two adventurers talked affably and laughed.

One was a dwarf, stroking his white beard, pounding his rotund belly, and helping himself to wine and food. And across from him was a lizardman, eating with his bare hands, his great, scaly body seated on a wine barrel. They drank the wine that was brought to them like water, in a manner that went beyond hearty and was practically celebratory.

"A blocker, a ranger, a warrior-priest, a cleric, a wizard. I would say we have a pretty good combination."

"Well, true."

Lizard Priest took a bite of the boar leg he held with both hands, while Dwarf Shaman lapped at a bit of wine that had spilled on the end of his beard. He poured wine from the bottle into his cup with a *glug, glug,* then slurped from the overflowing vessel. He downed it in a single gulp and let out a burp.

"Not enough in the front row, not enough in the back row, not enough connections to get equipment and items. Complain about everything, and you'll have everything to complain about."

"Just so, just so," Lizard Priest said, slapping the floor with his tail. "A party with three magic users is surely blessed."

"Got to admit, it is a little surprising."

"Your meaning…?"

"You." The red-faced dwarf thrust his empty cup in the direction of Lizard Priest. "At first…I thought you might not be interested in partying up with another cleric."

"Ha-ha-ha-ha-ha-ha! Oh, master spell caster. I never know what you will say next." Lizard Priest laughed easily. Finished with the meat, he gnawed on the leg bone, making a ferocious show of his teeth. "All of us alike have come from the dust of the sea, so there is no cause for me to be upset that a descendent of the rats leads us." Perhaps the alcohol was wearing off, for Dwarf Shaman looked weary as Lizard Priest rolled his eyes triumphantly. "I jest, I jest."

"Afraid I can't find it very funny," Dwarf Shaman said, waving away the lizard's nonchalance.

"Well, everyone has their own beliefs. If one chose to argue every time there was a difference, there would be no end."

"But heretics and Chaos followers are different, I suppose…?"

"That is no mere argument. They must be killed until there are none left."

Lizard Priest's head bobbed with utmost gravity; it was hard to tell how serious he was being.

Dwarf Shaman pushed back his empty plate, catching hold of a server to order some meat, and rested his chin in his hands.

"Just out of curiosity—you hear rumors about lizardmen. They're all left-handed, or their hearts are on the right. Is any of it true?"

"Hmm. I cannot speak to the location of my heart, but as for my hands, I would say I am ambidextrous." The idea that all lizardmen were left-handed because a god's left hand had created them was, apparently, nonsense.

Lizard Priest pointedly opened both of his clawed hands. Then he flicked his tongue as if he'd just thought of something.

"I hear dwarves can even float, from time to time."

"If we've got wine, there's nothing we can't do. Wine, and good food!"

Dwarf Shaman said the same thing from several months before and grinned.

§

"If you've got wine, there's nothing you can't do. Wine, and good food!"

Just like many adventurers' parties, theirs had been created at the tavern. At first, however, it had been just three people, and before that, only one.

The wind blew along the canal, making the air refreshingly cool as it came in through the door. It was twilight, and the water town tavern was alive with the sounds of voices giving toasts.

"But, m' honored uncle! Don't yeh think it's a bit much to ask, even from your nephew?"

Dwarf Shaman sounded most displeased. He crossed his arms firmly and turned his back.

Across from him was a dwarf with more muscles, more beard, and more wrinkles than him, sipping an ale with a fixed expression. At his seat was a well-used war hammer, along with a grasping hook. He was a shield breaker. The dwarf veteran's grim face, mug floating in front of it, eloquently bespoke the seriousness of the situation.

"Even so—listen. Right now, you are the only one I can call upon."

"But even for you, dear uncle—there's simply nothing to be done about it." Dwarf Shaman gulped down his ale and fixed his uncle with a lidded stare.

The dwarf's face had even more wrinkles than before, and he was starting to go bald. He was well and truly aging. It was understandable: one of the young people in his tribe had set off to pursue magic and was now acting the ruffian.

But even so…this!

"Go on an adventure with an elf?" Dwarf Shaman said. "One presumably chosen by their leader or their king or whoever?"

"Presumably."

"Tall, carved features, all too noble—practically shimmering with beauty—and oh so fragile."

"Most likely."

"Ever an elegant speaker, a first-rate poet, and the gods' gift to archery?"

"Well, I've not met them…"

"Gaaah!" *Absolutely no way, no how!* Dwarf Shaman waved his rough hands emphatically. He was not kidding. "I couldn't breathe around someone like that. I'd die of suffocation!"

"Listen, you selfish…"

"You say the world's in danger? I'm more than willing to help—but not with an elf!"

Then it happened. A cup came spinning through the air, trailing wine, and smacked Dwarf Shaman's uncle in the back of the head.

"Hey! You say that again!"

From behind his uncle, who was now facedown on the table and rubbing his head, there came a bracing, clear voice. Dwarf Shaman looked up and saw a sharp-eyed elf girl, her hands on her hips in an imposing stance. She was indeed delicate, willowy and modest-looking—and she wore close-fitting hunter's garb, her long ears flapping energetically. One would not have guessed it from her tone of voice, but her ears, longer than those of other elves, were proof that she was descended from the old high elves.

Expecting a fight, Dwarf Shaman grabbed his ax, more than happy to take part, but a dog-faced padfoot said, "I'll say it as many times as you want!"

The padfoot's furry skin made it hard to tell, but to judge by the expansive chest, it was probably a woman. And her rough but high-pitched voice made it seem likely that she was, in human terms, just a young adult. Probably not an adventurer. She was in good physical shape, her movements precise—signs of proper training. A soldier, most likely. She wiped off the wine that dribbled from her head and gave a snort.

"Elves just stay shut up in their forests, ignoring everything and everyone—and they're misers, to boot!"

"I'll show you the truth about elves!"

High Elf Archer hissed like a cat and threw herself at the dog-faced soldier. The table fell over with a crash, wine cups went flying, dishes were overturned. The drunks who had gathered in the tavern gave way at the familiar scene and started taking bets.

"My money's on the elf." "No, the padfoot." "But elves are so fragile." "Yeah, but padfoots are so stupid…"

"…What a troublemaker." *Oof, that hurt.* Dwarf Shaman shrugged at his uncle, who was rubbing his head and groaning.

"Rather unusual, for an elf."

"…Would you mind if your companion was someone like her?"

"Hrm, well. I don't suppose the high muckety-mucks of elfdom would pick someone so rash…"

As he muttered, Dwarf Shaman reached out for a plate. He grabbed a handful of dried beans, notwithstanding the wine splashed on them, popped them into his mouth, and crunched noisily.

Beside him, his uncle heaved a sigh. "They've already made their choice," he said. "And they picked her."

"Say what?"

"Look at the personal description."

His uncle pulled a rumpled piece of paper from his bag and passed it over. Dwarf Shaman opened it with fingers both thick and nimble, then held it up and looked through it at the fight.

"Ahh… That anvil…?"

If the haughty elves had chosen her, there was no reason to doubt her skills.

The elves resented the dwarves, but at the same time, they hated more than anything that the dwarves resented them.

But that's a little girl, or I'm a pebble.

She was shouting insults at the dog-muzzled soldier, the two of them pulling each other's hair and fur. The elves didn't exactly consider age unimportant, but he wondered if she was even a hundred years old.

"Still…" Give or take ten years—or a hundred—this was the elf who was to be his traveling companion. "…I think we'd break something trying to pull her out of that fight."

As he stroked his beard and considered what to do, Dwarf Shaman's eyes were drawn to the tavern door.

A huge shadow loomed there.

It was tremendous. Big as a boulder. Its broad movements were large, as were its jaws.

Now, where were those clothes from? Ah, yes. The heavily forested south.

The lizardman took one look at the brouhaha and rolled his eyes in his head. He entered the tavern with a shuffling gait and headed to the counter, oblivious to the looks of those around him. He did not try to sit in a chair, perhaps because of his huge size, or perhaps because of the tail that dragged on the floor.

"Many pardons, but I wish to wait for someone. As I do not know when they will arrive, I could be waiting for some time."

His voice was craggy as a stone. It was impressive that the long tongue within his jaws could maneuver around the common language so readily.

"Uh, sure," the tavern owner said with an awkward nod.

The lizard replied, "Splendid," with a nod of his own. "I await a dwarf and an elf. If any of your adventurers here fit that description, perhaps you could alert me."

Overhearing this, Dwarf Shaman glanced at his uncle, who said calmly, "I did hear a lizardman would be lending us his strength." It sounded as if he himself couldn't quite believe it.

"How now, dear uncle? Don't know his face?"

"Even if they gave me a description, I couldn't tell one lizardman from another."

"I suppose not."

The lizardmen, who proclaimed themselves descended from the fearsome nagas who had crawled out of the sea, were the most powerful warriors to be found in all the world.

They were opponents to make the blood run cold. They killed their enemies, massacred them, ate their hearts. Some disdained them as barbarians, and there were in fact—so it was said—some who had allied themselves with the forces of Chaos.

Regardless, this one was presumably on the side of Order.

But even so…

"Ahh, and a meal, if you would be so kind." The lizard priest held up a scaly finger. He remained standing at the counter; perhaps his tail got in the way when he tried to sit down. When his eyes spun and his jaws opened, his comment seemed lighthearted. "Regrettably, I carry no money, so I would repay you through labor—washing dishes or chopping firewood. You do not mind?"

Dwarf Shaman suddenly laughed. He took a drink of wine, pounded his belly, and gave a great, thick laugh. He laughed until the lizard priest turned his long neck to look in a most uncanny manner, and then the dwarf took a gulp of wine.

"Hey, Scaly!" he called to Lizard Priest. He let out a cough, then wiped the wine from his beard with one hand. "You see that long-eared girl fighting over there? Get her by the scruff of her neck and bring her over here, would you?"

Dwarf Shaman laughed easily, pointing to the elf, who was flailing atop the padfoot, oblivious to the goings-on around her. Presently, the padfoot had her by the hair and was rolling her into a new position. Hands and feet and nails were everywhere. Her elven dignity was gone. She was just a child in a fight.

"You do that, and I'll treat you to all the wine and meat you like."

"Oh-ho!" Lizard Priest's tail gave the ground a powerful slap. The owner frowned; so did Dwarf Shaman's uncle. "Very well, so I shall. Consider me grateful. Ah, virtue does beget virtue."

Immediately Lizard Priest, tail and all, jumped into the fray with a speed that belied his size. Beside Dwarf Shaman, grinning widely at the anarchy in the tavern, his uncle groaned. He seemed to have a stomachache. Even a mouthful of wine didn't appear to do him any good.

At length, the man who had been a shield breaker in the dwarven army for more than ten years said, "...If you'll excuse me, I'll be getting back to my unit." He left a handful of gold coins on the table and jumped unsteadily down from a chair built for human height.

He could not decide whether it was wise to leave the fate of his race in the hands of this party—including his nephew.

Oh, the commands of the gods...

As he tottered away from the tavern, the old shield breaker's head was filled with the sound of rolling dice.

§

"...Whaddayawant?"

Her hair was everywhere, her clothes were dirty, her cheeks were a bit swollen, and she had her back turned to him with an expression of disgust. Dwarf Shaman allowed himself a gleeful smile at this first sound out of the high elf's mouth.

"Who, me? I thought we might talk about work." He smirked and rubbed his thick hands together, *fsh-fsh-fsh.*

If she would at least sit facing me like an adult, I would feel like she was listening to me.

Fights must have been as common as bread and butter at this tavern, because the atmosphere had already relaxed again, the chatter and banter returning to life.

The badly bruised padfoot was in a corner seat, looking unhappy and tearing into a chunk of meat. With the fight having burned itself out, the erstwhile gamblers soon settled back down.

"Hm. In that case, there is something of considerable importance which I must first ask you."

The restored order of the tavern was partly thanks to the swift intervention of the lizardman, who now used a cask of wine in place of a chair. It had been quite a sight to see him take the elf and the padfoot each by the scruff of the neck and wrench them apart, but it was also an outcome no one had placed a bet on. So only the bookmaker made any profit, and the rhea went around the bar cheerfully waving his wine.

"And what's that, Scaly?"

Lizard Priest gave an "Mmm" and an immensely somber nod. "Could we perhaps consider our spending on food to be separate from the reward for this quest?"

"But of course," Dwarf Shaman said with a tug of his beard and a smile. "We'll send my honored uncle the tab."

"Most appreciated," Lizard Priest said, then opened his jaws wide and sunk them into a hunk of bone-in meat on the table.

High Elf Archer watched them, still puffing out her cheeks a bit. "So," she muttered, "what's this work? Not that I haven't heard the basics."

"Ah, yes, about that." Dwarf Shaman nodded, picked up a cup, and drained it. Then he used the empty vessel to shove aside some plates and make a space for himself. "You know about the battle that's going on over at the Capital with the Demon Lord or whoever it is?"

It was a rhetorical question. He drew a scroll from his bag and opened it on the table. It had been drawn with dyes on bark. The abstract yet precise picture marked it as an elven map. It depicted an ancient-looking building, smack in the middle of a wasteland.

"A council of war was about to be called, but then they found out there was a bunch of goblins living just behind them."

"A goblin nest, isn't that what it's called?"

"Yes, and a plenty big one, too."

Here. High Elf Archer looked where Dwarf Shaman was pointing and blinked. She peered at the symbol on the ancient building in the middle of the wasteland, then at the huge forest not far from it.

"Hey—that's my home!"

"Mm. That would explain why you're here..."

Lizard Priest nibbled more meat off his bone, chewed several times, and swallowed before speaking further.

"...Is this what you call politics?"

"Indeed." Dwarf Shaman nodded firmly. Well, this was a fine mess. One of their members was here to satisfy someone's honor. He smelled trouble ahead. "My uncle may think it's unreasonable, but we can't let the humans sit by while our armies are the only ones to mobilize."

"And no rheas or padfoots?"

High Elf Archer's ears twitched at the mention of the beast folk. The dog-faced soldier she had been fighting with had been brought to heel by a superior officer who had come rushing in. While the officer was tugging on the long face of the soldier, she had wondered whether such treatment was an everyday occurrence, or if dog people simply, by their nature, found it difficult to go against their superiors.

In any event, the water town was a beautiful city, but they did not feel threatened.

"I don't think we can expect more than some volunteers from them."

There were individual rheas of great bravery, but this did not extend to their clans or their administrators. At bottom, they adored peace and quiet, and they had little interest in anything that did not concern their homeland directly.

The padfoots were padfoots; they were so diverse that it was hard to quickly unite all of them behind any one cause. When they gathered, depending on which tribe seized leadership, things could go very well or very poorly. This was true even regarding the Demon Lord's awakening and subsequent war against all who had words on the continent. Granted, if the danger grew near enough, they would unite and rise up on their own...

"Our other problem is, we have to get a human to join us."

"Ah! I know a good one." High Elf Archer glanced up from the map. She held up her long, slim pointer finger, drawing a circle in the air. "He's called Orcbolg. A warrior who slays goblins on the frontier."

"What, you mean Beard-cutter?"

"Right. You dwarves might not know it, but right now, there's a very popular song about him going around."

She didn't actually know if the song was popular or not, but she needed a chance to look smart.

The Goblin King has lost his head to a Critical Hit most dire!

Blue blazing, Goblin Slayer's steel shimmers in the fire.

Thus, the King's repugnant plan comes to its fitting end, and lovely princess reaches out to her rescuer, her friend.

But he is Goblin Slayer! In no place does he abide, but sworn to wander, shall not have another by his side.

'Tis only air within her grasp the grateful maiden finds—the hero has departed, aye, with never a look behind.

As she finished humming the tune, she made a proud sound and stuck out her little chest.

"You don't know it because you've literally been living under a rock. That's dwarves for you."

"A fine thing for someone who stays shut up in her forest to say."

Dwarf Shaman gave her a dour look as she waved her ears in self-satisfaction.

I assume that song's only half the truth. It was always the best opinion to have about a bard's melodies.

"But, ahh, ahem."

This long-eared elf girl must be a ranger or a scout. The lizardman was a priest…a kind of warrior-monk, most likely. He himself knew magic, of course, and he also understood how to handle a weapon. But they did not have enough fighters.

He couldn't say for sure until he saw the man, but this *was* someone who'd had a song written about him. It was reasonable to assume he had a fair amount of skill.

"…That's good enough."

"The reward will be divided equally, then. Are we also agreed that we shall assume milord Goblin Slayer will join our company?"

Lizard Priest took in the party with a roll of his eyes. Dwarf Shaman and High Elf Archer both nodded.

At that, the lizardman said, "Then let us plan," and touched the tip of his nose with his tongue.

"First, this town," Dwarf Shaman said, casting his eye over the map. "Which town did you say he was in?"

"Well, uhh, I asked the bard, and..." High Elf Archer's pale finger searched across the elven map. Finally it found the frontier town, and she tapped the spot with a well-manicured nail. "Maybe around here?"

"That is not far distant. However... Even so." Lizard Priest seemed immensely serious as he looked over the map. "We seek to foil our enemy's plans. I believe we can assume this will provoke a reprisal."

"Hm? We may be attacked in the middle of an adventure, you mean?"

"Let us settle this now to avoid that possibility. Before they have a chance to consolidate their forces."

"Just leave it to us!" *Bop.* High Elf Archer made a fist and pounded her small chest with fervor. "The fate of the world hanging in the balance? That's when adventurers do their best work!"

"Hey, now," Dwarf Shaman said, goggling. "You know this isn't a game, right?"

"Sure I do. I don't know about you dwarves, but the elves have always used their bows to keep the world safe."

"Oh-ho. You don't say." The spell caster's eyes widened just a little; he gave a tug on his beard and sighed. "So that anvil of a chest of yours, it's so nothing interferes with drawing your bow?"

"Anvil?"

"It's hard...and flat."

"Why, you—!"

Embarrassment and anger sent blood rushing to the archer's cheeks. There was a clatter as she stood up from her chair and planted her hands on the table as she leaned out across it.

"That's some nerve! This when you dwarves—uhh, um..." She hung there, her mouth working open and closed. Her ears fluttered up and down, and her fingertip traced an aimless path in the air. "R-right! Those bellies! Your stomachs would make a drum look slim!"

"I'll have you know we call it being solidly built! A dwarf prefers this kind of body…" Dwarf Shaman pointedly cut himself off, then glanced at the elf out of the corner of his eye. "…Whatever you elves might like."

High Elf Archer could hardly fail to notice his gaze on her own chest. She crossed her arms with a deliberate snort, making her displeasure clear.

"I always knew dwarves had a warped sense of beauty!"

"Who is it that comes to buy our metalwork? Oh, right. Elves."

"So what?!"

And they were fighting. Other people in the tavern watched this age-old rivalry between the races play out in front of their eyes. But the atmosphere soon changed. Fights and arguments were a dime a dozen.

"Five silvers on the dwarf!" "A gold coin on the elf!" "Do it, girl!" "Spank her good, old man!"

Lizard Priest shook his head and heaved a sigh. Then he let out a great hiss. At the overpowering sense of a reptile on the hunt, the two adventurers shut their mouths. Lizard Priest nodded.

"Mm."

Good.

§

The carriage left the gate, cloaked by night. At this hour, anyone but adventurers would have found it safer to travel with a caravan or the like. But the three of them did not have the time, and their hand had been forced in more ways than one.

The vehicle they were in was not a very good one, just a slightly modified cargo hauler. And the horse was just average…well, maybe a bit below average. Dwarf Shaman and Lizard Priest had the reins. High Elf Archer was watching the sky, her bow at the ready.

Traveling by carriage meant going faster than a person could walk, but slower than a horse could run. Dwarf Shaman was not pleased with this situation. He had wanted to get the best possible ride and horse, to say nothing of the driver. But the funds he had gotten from his uncle were limited, as was their time. He had had to compromise.

"And to top it all off, we have to go slowly. What a lot of trouble."

"Bear in mind that we do not have the luxury of changing horses at one of the intermediate stations." Seated beside him on the driver's platform, Lizard Priest replied to Dwarf Shaman's cautious comment to himself. "And if you consider the trouble we would have if we were to rush and thereby attract unwelcome attention, this way is in fact faster."

"Unwelcome attention?" High Elf Archer tilted her head, flicking the tips of her ears in the direction of the coachman's seat.

"Bandits or brigands, I suppose."

"Right..."

Her face scrunched at the reply, as if she found it very unpleasant. Dwarf Shaman caught the plain display of emotion in his peripheral vision and made a sound of annoyance.

"We managed somehow in town, by the auspices of that lovely lady, but now we're out in the open fields."

"Once away from the sanctuary of the Supreme God, it may be only a matter of time until some ill spirit sets upon us," said Lizard Priest.

"Are you talking about what they call god's blessing? Our god of smithing and steel is only good for courage in battle..." Nonetheless, Dwarf Shaman muttered a prayer to the great god Krome. He shrugged and shook his head, saying without malice, "Got to at least pray that our elf girl doesn't lose her nerve when it counts."

"Hrk...!" The elf's ears could hardly miss this nasty little comment. "Just you watch! You'll bow down to thank me when this is over!"

"Ahh, sure. Can't say I've got my hopes up." He waved an open palm. High Elf Archer gave a furious snort and rolled onto her back. Dwarf Shaman took his cue from her, looking up at the sky. It was full of stars, and the two moons. The stars sparkled as if someone had scattered precious jewels over black velvet. The moons shone like a pair of eyes, green and cold.

Perhaps it was the approaching summer that gave the air its unusual dampness and made it seem hard to breathe.

"I could do with just a breeze..." High Elf Archer muttered. Dwarf Shaman felt the same, though he said nothing.

Their party arrived at an abandoned plot of earth that seemed once to have been a village. The gloomy skeletons of houses in the moonlight cast obscene shadows on the road. This corpse of the village had gone wild, left to the overgrowth; it would have seemed desolate even in daylight. Now, at night, it would not have been surprising to find ghosts or ghouls there…

"Hr-ah?"

High Elf Archer made a strange sound. She looked over her shoulder, her nose tickling.

"What is it now? Stopping to sniff the flowers or something? Hm?"

"Oh, stop. There's a weird smell…" She waved her hand in front of her nose, casting a glance around the area with an expression of deep suspicion. "It's…kind of thick, and kind of prickly… And I can smell it even though there's no wind."

"…Sulfur, most likely."

"This is sulfur?"

"Some kind of vapor mixed with sulfur, to be more precise."

What that meant was not lost on any of them. They went silent and gave a collective gulp. The elf looked up, an anxious expression on her face.

"Above us!"

It appeared less like a living thing and more like a machine, flesh in the shape of a man-made bug. Its body was red, its head spiked as if it were wearing a hat. A red cap.

It flapped its batlike wings, and cruel, curved claws were visible on its hands.

A lesser demon. And there were two of them. This was a random encounter.

"Are they coming?!" shouted Dwarf Shaman, giving a crack of the reins and urging the horse on. The animal whinnied, having sensed things not of this world. The clacking carriage wheels began spinning in earnest as the horse set off at full tilt.

"Make him go faster…! No, give me the reins. You prepare your spells!"

"All yours!"

Nearly flinging the reins at Lizard Priest, Dwarf Shaman spun around in his seat. He was careful, of course, to hold tight to the shoulder strap of his bag of catalysts, lest it go flying away.

"Can't we get away?" High Elf Archer said, licking her lips as her bow sang out with arrow after arrow.

"Don't know about that, but—" Dwarf Shaman said.

"We cannot risk information getting out," Lizard Priest said with a deep nod, as calmly as if he were getting ready to eat dinner. "We must kill them here."

The demons appeared to have the same idea. With a rush of air, one of them dove at the carriage. As someone shouted out that initiative had been taken, there was a crash, and splinters of wood went flying.

The demon had swiped at the carriage from behind, its claws as deadly as any weapon.

"Ergh! Pfah!" Dwarf Shaman brushed bits of carriage out of his beard and bellowed, "If you ruin this thing, we'll be the ones who take the blame!"

"I shall see to the safety of the horse, so if you would be so kind..." Lizard Shaman replied.

The next attack came from the sky as they chatted.

A rushing dive, wings folded. High Elf Archer glowered; the creature had a moon at its back. Her ears jumped, reading the wind, her drawn bowstring creaking.

"You stupid, stinking...!"

"AAARREMMEERRRR?!?!"

An otherworldly scream ensued. High Elf Archer had not missed her chance to fire. The demon, its hand nailed to the carriage by the arrow, writhed about, tearing up the wood with its claws.

"That'll show you!"

The last thing the demon ever saw was an elf drawing her bow directly in front of it, the arrow tipped with a bud.

The bowstring made a sound that would have suited a high-quality musical instrument; it launched the arrow through the demon's eyeball and into its brain. The creature's neck snapped backward under the force of the blow. The corpse hung limply, scraping along the ground. High Elf Archer gave a smile of appreciation for her handiwork. "That's one down!"

"Fine work! But as he is something of a burden, perhaps you could see him off our carriage?"

"Yeah, sure…guh, what?!"

In the space of an instant, several strands of High Elf Archer's hair were caught by a claw and went dancing through the air. The monster that had come racing down had taken a swipe at her neck. High Elf Archer fell on her behind, trembling, still holding the shaft of the arrow she had pulled out. At the same moment, the dead demon slid to the ground, bouncing with a dull thump.

"Bit of a fright, there?"

"I'm not scared, I'm angry!"

She bristled at the tease from Dwarf Shaman, whose hand had been ready with his bag of catalysts the entire time, then glared up at the sky. With one fewer demon corpse on board, their speed was picking up again—but it was no match for a creature with wings.

"You, dwarf!" High Elf Archer shouted without taking her eyes off the air. "Can't you use a spell to knock him out of the sky or something?"

"I guess I could, in so many words…" He closed one eye and peered up, judging the speed and distance between him and the enemy. The curtain of night was powerless before the light of the moons and stars, and dwarves could see easily through darkness anyway. "It's just that if I brought him down with a spell, he'd only get back up again."

"What?! Some spell caster! Stupid, stupid dwarf!"

"Aw, quit your whinin'," Dwarf Shaman said coldly, frowning. "They don't move by the same laws we do. Steel and iron are the ways to deal with them."

"Physically, you mean. Well spoken!" Holding the reins, Lizard Priest twisted his huge jaws into a smile that reminded them of nothing so much as a shark. He seemed to do some quick calculations, then nodded in satisfaction. "Master spell caster, you say you can bring it down?"

"I should think," Dwarf Shaman nodded. "Not for very long, though."

"Then master ranger, kindly pretend you are going to take a high shot…"

"Can do!"

Without waiting to hear the rest of the plan, High Elf Archer loosed

an arrow into the night. It was potent as magic, an arrow as only an elf could fire one, but the demon nimbly zigged out of the way.

"Aw, damn!" High Elf Archer clicked her tongue and nocked a new arrow into her bow, drawing the string.

"Now, then," Lizard Priest said, tugging on the reins to slow the horse to a crawl. "Perhaps you would be so kind as to pierce him with an arrow tied to a rope?"

"An arrow tied to a rope...?!" High Elf Archer took the rope that had been tossed onto the cargo platform, her mouth a flat line as she gazed up at the enemy. The red-skinned monster continued to beat its wings, looking for its opportunity to come at them. "Fine, I'll do it!"

No sooner had she spoken than she began to tie the rope to the arrow. The elf's agile fingers had no trouble, even atop a rocking carriage. She kept her eyes and ears on the opponent, her hands moving as if someone else were controlling them. Her mouth relaxed. "You're like a general or something," she said.

"You are too kind." Lizard Priest gave a broad shake of his head. "If you must compare me to something, I am like the feather on a shaft. I only set the direction, I do not..." Before continuing, his tongue flicked out and touched the tip of his nose. "Mm," he said at length. "To have a functioning unit, one must gather an arrow head, a shaft, a feather, a bow, and an archer."

Ahh. High Elf Archer smiled faintly. That was a metaphor she could understand. "I wonder if that would make me the tip. Come on, dwarf, make sure that spell's on target!"

"Hmph! That's quite enough out of you!"

As Dwarf Shaman shot back at High Elf Archer and got the enemy in his field of view, he noticed something: a single red light in the sky. It was burning in the wide, open mouth of the demon...

"Firebolt incoming!"

"Ahh, *now*!" Lizard Priest said with heartfelt joy, giving the reins a tremendous shake. The horse made an awful neigh of confusion and fear, and the carriage careened in a new direction, creaking all the while.

Just seconds later, a beam of flame lanced down at where the carriage would have been, embers flying into the sky. The glowing light illuminated Lizard Priest's terrible visage.

"Ha-ha-ha-ha-ha-ha-haaaa! Now things have become interesting!"

"I think you've mistaken our carriage for a chariot, Scaly!"

"Indeed," the lizard replied, provoking a "Nutter..." from Dwarf Shaman as he looked at the sky.

The red demon appeared to be readying for another dive, now that they had evaded its trademark firebolt.

Think it's going to be that easy, do you?

Dwarf Shaman bellowed at the shadow as it grew steadily larger.

"Pixies, pixies, hurry, quickly! No sweets for you—I just need tricksies!"

Words full of the true power to bend reality poured out, and the magic circle caught the demon cleanly.

Normally, the creature should never have been able to escape the chains of gravity, no matter how hard it flapped its wings. Lesser demons were still demons; these monsters lived to twist the natural order.

"ARREMERRRERRRR!!"

The demon, which had fallen to earth, howled and flapped its wings mightily, shattering the magical bonds that held it. It would have its revenge on that dwarf, and that lizardman, and that elf. The mere thought of the blood of an ancient high elf, the smell of her liver, was enough to stoke the greed of the base creature.

"Take this!"

It was an arrow from that very elf that put an agonizing end to that greed. She had leaned out, bracing herself against the edge of the carriage, and ruthlessly fired a single bud-tipped bolt into the monster.

"AREEERM?!"

Thrashing with torment, the demon was just a bit too slow in noticing the rope tied to the arrow. And that was all the time the carriage needed to pick up speed and pull the rope taut.

A hideous roar of despair, enough to make the blood run cold, echoed across the plain.

The demon could not have imagined that it would be dragged across the ground behind the carriage. There was a certain pitifulness to it as it bounced along, restrained by the party as it scrabbled at the dirt and tried desperately to fly.

Lesser demons were still strong. If the trio couldn't control its position, it would soon have its claws in the earth, and if it could stand, it would be only a moment until was in the air. And once aloft, it would be dangerous.

"What next?!" High Elf Archer shrieked, pulling another arrow out of her quiver.

Lizard Priest stood easily. "We strike the finishing blow, of course." He held one of his catalysts, a fang, pressed between his palms. *"O sickle wings of velociraptor, rip and tear, fly and hunt!"* A large Swordclaw grew and then sharpened in his hands.

"What about the horse?!" But when High Elf Archer glanced back, she saw a Dragontooth Warrior with a firm grip on the reins.

"Wait a second, Scaly," Dwarf Shaman said, his eyes going wide. "What's this business about the finishing blow? Y-you're not going to—"

"Jump? Do not be silly." Lizard Priest shook his head with a considered motion that must have come naturally to him as a monk. "That would be ridiculous."

In the next instant, the carriage groaned as Lizard Priest leaped at the lesser demon.

"O fearsome nagas! See my deeds, my great forebears!"

"AREEERMEER?!?!"

Claw, claw, fang, tail. He struck and slashed and tore at the demon as it struggled to resist him. The creature opened its jaws to let loose a firebolt, but Lizard Priest howled—"Grrrryaaahhh!"—and aimed a kick directly at its throat, crushing its windpipe. And then his Swordclaw found the demon's head, lopping it off effortlessly.

The head went rolling across the ground and disappeared into the grass. The rest of the body, still attached to the carriage, trailed a spray of bluish-purple blood. Lizard Priest, standing atop the corpse, was quite calm despite the growing amount of blood covering him; he lifted his head happily.

"Ahh, I have earned merit this day."

The sun had begun to peek over the horizon, and its rays cloaked Lizard Priest with an indescribable atmosphere.

§

"Look at this. Didn't we secretly agree that we weren't going to go against him?"

"Ah, but betimes my blood boils." After Lizard Priest's straightforward answer, he gleefully raised a block of cheese in both hands. He opened his mouth and tore into it, each bite accompanied by a cry of "Sweet nectar!" and a slap of his tail on the floor. "For I am a warm-blooded creature, you see."

"Your jokes never make any sense to me," Dwarf Shaman grumbled. He threw up his hands in resignation, but also to signal to the waitress that he wanted more ale. When drinking with friends, Dwarf Shaman felt it was only polite to fill his barrel of a belly as full as he could.

"So are we all together?"

"I don't take your meaning."

"Your arrow. Arrow and bow."

"Ahh." Lizard Priest swallowed the well-masticated lump of cheese with a great gulp and licked the crumbs from his lips. "The arrowhead is our ranger, the shaft that holds us together is you, master spell caster, and I am the feather…"

"…The bow is that girl, and Beard-cutter would be the archer—is that right?"

"Just so, just so."

Dwarf Shaman took the ale the waitress brought him, watching Lizard Priest nod out of the corner of his eye. He brought the brimming cup to his mouth and took a sip, then downed it in a single gulp.

"However renowned an archer, if he shoots only at the sky he will come to harm one day."

"Then again, if we hunt nothing but goblins, is that good or bad?" Dwarf Shaman, red-faced, let out a burp and ran a hand through his beard to wipe off some droplets.

"Whatever the case…" Lizard Priest began.

"Indeed, in any case," Dwarf Shaman concurred.

"It is a fine party."

"No complaints here."

Lizard Priest smiled with his great jaws, and Dwarf Shaman let out a rumbling belly laugh. The two of them took the fresh cups that had been brought to them, and smacked them together.

"To good friends."

"To good companions in battle."

"To good adventures!"

Hear, hear! By the time the cups had been raised three times, they were empty.

How many times do we meet, and part?
Some vanish, to ash, as we must
With the hope of reunion does each journey start
Like flipping a page that is turning to dust
Remember the legend who trained many years?
What was his name? Now I cannot recall
You realize too late, now he's no longer here
And though we have partings and meetings withal
Each such encounter is once, and that's all.

So night deepened for the adventurers.

CHAPTER 10

Of Going There and Back Again

Evening was encroaching as the shared carriage came to its stop. The sinking sun threw out its last red rays, and the world was painted purple alongside streaks of darkness. The vehicle's stretching shadow merged with the huge, warped silhouettes of the town, creating cartoonish and bizarre figures.

When he heard children racing home in the distance, Goblin Slayer relaxed. He did not understand why his muscles grew so stiff in the carriage, even though all he was doing was riding along. He was fully conscious, but his body felt heavy, his head fuzzy and his footsteps uncertain and light.

I suppose this is the moment, he decided, closing his eyes for a few seconds to push back the dull pain within them. He recalled hearing somewhere, once, that humans could only fight continuously for at best about twenty days. Without rest, any more than that would likely degrade their abilities in a number of ways.

Goblin Slayer was not so optimistic as to assume he could last that long.

He set off at a bold stride, making a beeline for the building that towered next to the main gate—the Guild. He would make his report, collect his reward, see to his equipment, get some rest, and then go out once more to kill goblins.

It was the exact same routine he always followed. It never changed. It couldn't.

But as he went to open the Guild door…

"Whoa!"

"Oh…my."

It opened from the other side, and he found himself nearly running into a man and a woman coming out. The man jumped back a few steps when confronted with the steel helmet covered in crimson stains. His well-endowed female companion simply stood with her staff at the ready and her lips forming an elegant arch.

"Geez, pal," Spearman said with a tremendously tired expression. "You really need to stop walking around with that helmet on."

"Did I surprise you?"

"No more than usual!"

"You…know, you…look like living…armor, yes?"

Witch's giggling seemed to make the already nonplussed Spearman even more irate.

Goblin Slayer turned his helmet from one side to the other, watching them without concern. Spearman was equipped with his armor and his beloved spear, a knapsack hanging from the point. As for Witch, she was wearing her usual outfit and held her usual staff. She also carried a cylindrical container with a scroll in it. It was perfectly obvious where the two were going.

"Off on an adventure?"

"Yes." Witch's eyes, graced by long lashes, narrowed slightly. "A date…if you will."

"And I guess you've been up to goblin slaying?"

"Yes," Goblin Slayer nodded. "I just finished."

"Feh. Sure," Spearman muttered, then opened his mouth to say something else. But an expression that was difficult to describe passed over his face; he looked from the helmet to the Guild and back again, then closed his mouth without saying anything.

Goblin Slayer pushed the door open, making room to one side. After a moment's reflection, thinking he should say something, he offered briefly, "Be careful."

"You're the last person I want to hear that from."

Spearman bumped a fist against Goblin Slayer's shoulder as he passed by. He was already on his way as Goblin Slayer regarded his shoulder with a touch of perplexity. When he looked up again, he found Witch giving him an oddly significant smile before making her exit, her hips swaying.

"...Hmm."

Goblin Slayer cocked his head slightly, letting go of the half-open door. It creaked as it slid shut, and then he opened it again, by himself this time.

The rousing holler of the building enveloped him. One party was clustered at the front desk, trying to report on their adventure. Another eyed the bulletin board, looking for a quest they could start immediately. Some people were hanging out at the bar, enjoying a day off, while others were eagerly taking on new adventures. It was loud, it was rude, and the whole place rang with the sound of weapons and equipment and voices.

Goblin Slayer gave the scene a once-over from the entranceway, then strode over to the open waiting area. He could see that Guild Girl was currently busy helping other adventurers. His head bobbed in response to her slight bow, and he plopped onto the bench.

"Oh!"

"Ah!"

This provoked a pair of incoherent exclamations from nearby. He turned to look and found a young man and a young woman who appeared completely exhausted.

It was Rookie Warrior and Apprentice Priestess. Perhaps they had been having a water fight, because their hair was damp, and they were soaked through. All the same, there was a hint of excitement on their faces, most likely the pleasure of a job done.

A club hung next to the sword at the boy's hip. It was grimy and well-used, and there was a loop of string at the hilt. Goblin Slayer tilted his helmet ever so slightly.

"So you're using it."

"...Oh, uh, yeah." Rookie Warrior shifted uncomfortably, then gave the club a gentle smack with his open palm. "It's pretty good."

"Is that so?" Goblin Slayer said with a nod.

Rookie Warrior scratched his cheek in a way that suggested indecision, then said, "I've been thinking…"

"…"

"Maybe I'll name it Masher."

"I see."

"Hey," Apprentice Priestess said, giving the young warrior a jab with her elbow. "That name's embarrassing."

Rookie Warrior grunted, but didn't back down. "Yeah, but…"

Goblin Slayer looked from one to the other as they began to bicker, then stood up.

The party in front of Guild Girl was gone.

Goblin Slayer was silent for a moment, but before he began to move he murmured, "That's not bad."

Their argument stopped in an instant. The boy and girl gaped at the cheap-looking steel helmet as though they couldn't believe what they'd just heard. The helmet inclined just a bit to look down at them.

"It won't do for throwing, but that string is clever," the quiet voice went on. "Maybe I'll try it."

The two young adventurers found themselves looking at each other as Goblin Slayer turned his back to them and strode off.

At the reception desk Guild Girl, finished with the other adventurers, was straightening a sheaf of papers. When she saw the grimy steel helmet, she gave a bright smile.

"Welcome back, Mr. Goblin Slayer!"

"Thanks." The chair groaned under his weight as he sat down, and he briefly registered some unfamiliar objects on the reception desk. They were dolls small enough to fit in the palm of the hand—no, it was a group of five or six pawns in the shape of adventurers.

"Oh, these?" Guild Girl couldn't restrain a giggle as she patted one with a fingertip. It seemed to be a warrior in light armor. It stood with a tiny shield and sword, and she placed it gently in her hand. "I found them the other day… They're just game pieces, but I felt a little bad putting them away somewhere."

"Is that so?" She nodded at him and put the figurine back in its place. A lightly armored scout, a knight with a steel helmet, an elf sorceress, a dwarf warrior, and an elderly monk.

"Is this…a party?"

"Yes. Adventurers who set off to close the gate of the tomb that leads to hell. Not that they ever quite managed…" She scratched her cheek.

"It's well balanced," he said.

"Yes. It's a very good party." She talked about their adventure as if it had actually happened. How they had found the entrance to the tomb, fought with a guardian monster in green, and the terrible maze…

Goblin Slayer listened in silence, until Guild Girl came back to herself with a start.

"P-pardon me! I've just been going on all this time…"

"Don't worry," Goblin Slayer said with a shake of his head. "It's quite interesting."

"It is?" Guild Girl cocked her head with a slight bob of her braids. Then she gave a little cough. She offered him a cup of the tea she had prepared and settled herself again in her seat.

"So, uh… How'd your quest go?"

Goblin Slayer took the cup and drained it, then said:

"There were goblins."

Right, right. Guild Girl was smiling as if this made her happy, her pen dancing along the page. How many were there? How had they set themselves up? How had he killed them? Did he rescue anyone? Was the quest successful?

He gave her the information dispassionately. All was just as usual. Another goblin slaying job by Goblin Slayer. When she had finished taking down a quick report, she read it back over, double-checking everything.

It was all in order. Guild Girl congratulated him again on a job well done, then put her seal on the report. Now the job was truly over. All that was left was to get his reward from the safe.

"Now then, your reward… Oh, that's right." She clapped her hands with their neatly trimmed nails. There was something she mustn't forget. "Do you remember the village from the other day?"

"Which village?"

"The one you went to alone…"

"Ah," he nodded. The cave. The villagers. The boy. The prisoner. "I remember."

"Well, that village," Guild Girl said with a meaningful chuckle, "sent you a little thank-you gift."

She told him to wait for a moment and scuttled off like a happy puppy. She took a leather pouch out of the safe and measured it on a scale, making sure the gold weighed what it should. No problem.

She put the pouch on a tray, then gave a *hup!* and placed an incongruous basket beside it. The result, on the reception desk, was a pile of corn that looked to be freshly harvested.

"They said this is for you to eat!"

"Oh-ho."

Goblin Slayer picked up one of the ears; it was heavy in his hand. He pulled back the leaves to reveal beautiful golden kernels.

"This is very ripe."

"Isn't it?" She stuck out her delightfully average chest, as proud as if she had grown it herself. "And you know what? The person who brought it was someone you saved recently."

"...Was it, now?"

"Uh-huh!" Guild Girl let her eyes drift to the corn with an expression that bespoke relief. It was rare that adventurers or mercenaries found themselves with a second chance when they had failed once. "It's great, huh?"

"Yeah." Goblin Slayer let his helmet bob slowly up and down. "Excellent."

And then, with all the paperwork and procedures finished, Goblin Slayer took the basket of corn and stood. Except for very recent registrants, none of those gathered in the Guild paid him special attention. Perhaps a few glanced up and remarked, "Oh, he's at it again." It was no different for Apprentice Boy as he peeked out from the workshop, offering a small bow.

Goblin Slayer stopped. "What is it?" The boy wiped his hands on his apron before he spoke.

"Aw, nothing. I just thought you might, uh, need a sword or something, and I wanted to come take your order."

"I see," Goblin Slayer nodded. "In that case, one, please."

"Sure thing. Don't want to order several at once?"

"No." Goblin Slayer patted the sheath at his side. "I can only carry one at a time."

"That's our Goblin Slayer," Apprentice Boy said with a wry smile and a nod. "I'll get one ready for you, then, and—whoa! That's some corn!" He caught sight of the basket and blinked. "Lucky you," he said. "I didn't realize it was the season already."

"It is."

"Out in the country, back before I came here, we used to boil corn all the time. You know, in summer."

"Is that so?" Goblin Slayer reached nonchalantly into the basket and pulled out two or three ears of corn. He thrust them in the apprentice's direction. "Do you want some?"

Apprentice Boy made a sound of surprise. "Can I? Really?"

"I owe quite a bit to you and your master."

"W-well, sure, then! Thanks very much!" Bowing his head, Apprentice Boy ran off with corn under both arms. "Hey, boss!" His voice echoed in the workshop. Goblin Slayer turned and walked on.

The day was ending and adventures were over, so the Guild was packed with adventurers. He worked his way through the crowd, giving a slight nod of his head each time someone he knew greeted him.

"Geez. You could have let us know. We could have cooked them in the kitchen."

Just as he reached the door, he felt a tugging on his elbow.

"What?" He looked and saw Padfoot Waitress, holding his arm and glaring pointedly in the direction of the workshop.

"In fact, I'm pretty sure you should have brought us some of that first."

"You think so?"

"Yeah. We could have prepared it, and everyone could have shared it! That wasn't very nice of you..." she continued, piling on the invective.

Goblin Slayer simply nodded and said, "Is that so?"

With his basket of corn, the steel-helmeted adventurer stood out like an even sorer thumb than usual.

"Yo, Goblin Slayer!" a jubilant voice called from the tavern.

He turned his helmet to look. Heavy Warrior waved a hand, his red face suggesting he was well into his cups already.

"You look like a man who needs a drink. C'mere and let's toast!"

"Don't tell me you want *him* to join us?" Female Knight, her lovely face tinged with a bit of crimson, puffed out her cheeks next to the warrior.

"Aw, what's the harm? Just once in a while."

"Some of us would like something other than goblin stories to go with our drinks." Her chair clattered as she stood with an exasperated mutter of "Oh, forget it," and changed seats. "Move over, kids. The paladin's sitting here."

"I dunno, you really think you can call yourself a paladin with a mouth like that…?" said Scout Boy.

"You watch yourself. See if I don't Holy Smite you one of these days…"

"Sure. It's been nothing but Shield Bash with you lately," Druid Girl commented.

"And what, pray tell, is wrong with a knight using her shield? Blame the gods for not giving me any miracles!"

"Agh, will you will be quiet already?! A man can't hear himself think!"

Scout Boy and Druid Girl had started arguing like children when Female Knight pushed them out of the way. Heavy Warrior broke in and glowered at everyone. He had no attention to spare for Goblin Slayer.

Just as the latter was trying to figure out what to do, a shadow appeared beside him. It was the half-elf from Heavy Warrior's party. He offered an elegant bow of his head and winked.

"I will have a word with our esteemed leaders. Please, pay them no mind."

"No kidding!" Padfoot Waitress said with a chuckle. "They're waaay past drunk. Nothing to see there." She waved her paw-like hand as if shooing something away. "All right, sir, off with you. It wouldn't do to keep anyone waiting, would it?"

"…" Goblin Slayer turned his helmet toward both of them, then toward Heavy Warrior at the bar. He looked up, then down. "Thanks."

"No problem!" She answered his quiet word of gratitude with a smile, and he said nothing further as he left the building.

Jostled by the adventurers all around, he opened the saloon doors and went outside. There was a cool night breeze, and within his helmet, Goblin Slayer closed his eyes. Then he took a step forward. He proceeded down the street with his usual bold, casual stride, heading for the main gate. Then again, the gate was right next to the Guild, so it wasn't very far. Still…

Among the press of adventurers and travelers hurrying through the gate, one massive form stood head and shoulders above the rest. Goblin Slayer stopped when he noticed the distinctive silhouette, and its owner saw him, too.

"Oh-ho, milord Goblin Slayer!" The lizardman's face lit up, and he made a broad wave of his arm to get the warrior's attention. When Goblin Slayer got close enough through the crowd, he could see three others at the lizard's side—all his usual companions were there.

The four looked exhausted, their clothes dirty, but a sense of accomplishment was clear on their faces. Dwarf Shaman's nose twitched at the faint smell of blood, and he unstoppered a bottle of wine to get rid of it.

"What's this? Don't tell me you're heading out again at this hour, Beard-cutter?"

"No," Goblin Slayer said with a shake of his helmet. "I'm on my way home. What about you?"

"Just wrapped up a little adventure."

"It's sure rough with just one person on the front row!" High Elf Archer made a sound of annoyance and an exaggerated shrug, shaking her head. Then she reached out and grabbed Priestess, pulling her into a hug.

"E-eek!"

"I'll bet you're pretty tired."

"N-no, I'm—" The sudden physical contact seemed to throw her for a loop; it might or might not have been why she lowered her head shyly. "I'm fine. Thanks to everyone working so hard to protect me…"

"Aw, and modest, too!" High Elf Archer held the girl's willowy arms, patting her head and chirping, "What a sweetie." She managed to look up at Goblin Slayer at the same time, with no apparent intention of letting him get away. "Now," she said, "I'm no dwarf, but I thought we should have a little treat."

"I see."

"Ooh, is that corn?" The elf's eyes, ever sharp, fell on the basket Goblin Slayer was carrying. Unless she was terribly mistaken, it was full of ripe, yellow corn, still in the leaf. "Ooh! Ooh! Can I have some? Please?" No sooner had she spoken than she had let go of Priestess and snatched an ear.

"Are you an elf or a rhea?" Dwarf Shaman asked, caught between exasperation and amusement.

"It's fine," Goblin Slayer said, causing the elf to puff out her little chest even more proudly.

Priestess was busy being frantic at the whole situation, and Lizard Priest let out a sharp hiss. "Oh-ho. This was a staple in my homeland."

"Huh? You mean you eat something besides meat?" Priestess asked, surprised. She could see an argument coming on despite their fatigue, and she wanted to avoid it if at all possible.

"We often made porridge from it or drank it in a soup with honey or agave."

"Wow! I can hardly picture it." High Elf Archer leaned in, her interest successfully diverted, and Priestess let out a small sigh of relief.

"In that case, I shall prepare some. Ah, yes, milord Goblin Slayer."

"What?"

"If I may trouble you, I would like another round of…"

"Cheese?"

"…Mm."

Lizard Priest's head bobbed restlessly, and he couldn't hold back a slap of his tail on the ground.

"I'll have it delivered directly to your room."

"Ahh! My gratitude knows no bounds! This has become an addiction with me…" He went on in this vein, with cries of "Oh, sweet nectar!" and the like.

"Orcbolg," High Elf Archer said, watching the lizard out of the corner of her eye, "why don't you just bring it yourself, then?"

"Then it would not be farm work."

"Hmmm."

Did that count as a kind of integrity? High Elf Archer flicked her ears and giggled. "That's perfect, then…I was just thinking of asking you to do some work."

"Goblins?"

"Absolutely not," High Elf Archer said with a wave of her ears. "I want you to see this girl back to the temple."

"Hwah?!" Priestess had not expected to become the subject of conversation. She found herself being pushed from behind until she was standing in front of Goblin Slayer. She looked frantically from him to High Elf Archer and back. "Oh! Uh! I—I'm fine…by myself. It's not far…"

"The open road's a dangerous place at night." Dwarf Shaman ran a hand along his beard, a teasing smile on his face. "Goblins could show up at any time. Isn't that right, Beard-cutter?"

"Yes," Goblin Slayer said with utmost seriousness. "But aren't you staying at the Guild inn?"

"Yeah, but it sounds like she's got something to do with the autumn festival, hmm?"

When High Elf Archer looked at her for confirmation, Priestess seemed unable to form an answer. It was true, apparently, but admitting as much would mean being escorted back to the temple.

Lizard Priest cornered her further, adding his voice to the chorus: "You would do well to let him accompany you."

"T'aint the time to be shy now, lass."

"…"

Everyone sounded so serious. They couldn't be wrong, could they? Priestess looked from one to another, hoping to find some hint in their faces, when Goblin Slayer started moving.

"Let's go." And he strode off with those two blunt words.

"Oh, um, uh, y-yes, sir!" Priestess found herself scurrying after him, anxious not to be left behind.

She glanced over her shoulder to find the other three watching them go, their smiles suggesting they were amused by the scene. She found that strangely embarrassing and felt the heat rising in her cheeks, but she bowed to them just the same.

"I'll, uh, see you tomorrow then!"

Goblin Slayer stopped and thought for a moment, his helmet tilting just a little, then started walking again. Priestess hurried to catch up as he got farther and farther away. She only caught up to him when he slackened his pace.

"H-have you been, uh, busy recently?" Priestess gazed up at him, struggling to bring her breathing under control. He wore the same steel helmet as always. If the headgear had not already concealed his expression, the darkness would have.

"Yes," Goblin Slayer said with a nod. "I needed some money."

"Money…?"

"I've saved enough now."

Hm. Priestess tapped a pale finger to her lips, watching the ground in thought. She felt a touch of dissatisfaction, and a touch of worry. She didn't experience it as jealousy, exactly. It was a sadness, almost an anger, that he hadn't called upon her. He should have felt free to let her know.

As she stood thinking, he kept walking, and she made an effort to catch up. It didn't take them long to reach the temple of the Earth Mother.

"We're here." When Goblin Slayer called out, she looked up to find herself at the doorway to the temple. The purple sun of twilight played across the porcelain walls; within, a fire lit by the night watch flickered.

"Thank you very much," Priestess said, walking up the stairs to the entrance.

Am I…okay with this?

No. No, she wasn't. That was why she plucked up her courage and spoke. She was sure her face was red, but perhaps between the twilight and the darkness, he wouldn't be able to tell.

"U-um! Next time you go on an adventure, be…be sure to let me know!" she said as forcefully as she could.

"…"

Goblin Slayer said nothing at first and only looked at her. But after a moment he said, "All right," and gave an unmistakable nod. "I will."

That was all Priestess needed to hear. Her face lit up so brightly it was obvious even in the deepening dark. "Okay!" she exclaimed. "See you tomorrow, then!"

"See you tomorrow," he murmured, watching as she turned and disappeared into the temple.

For a while he simply stood there in front of the building.

I met quite a few people today. He'd had the thought once before.

But, he reflected, it wasn't exactly true. Those people were always there. Things had, in some sense, changed. But in another, they hadn't. It was simply that he had never noticed it.

He had the sense that a great many things had escaped his notice. He took a deep breath in and then let it slowly out.

He walked past the Guild—still bustling—then out the gate and onto the road. The twin moons and the stars between them conspired to mute the sense of darkness, even though it was night. A breeze rustled the underbrush, offering a pleasant coolness.

He walked silently down the path at his usual pace.

And then, in the distance, he saw a single point of light. At the same time, in the same place as always. He had come to where he could see the light of the farm.

Goblin Slayer picked up his pace slightly. He passed the stone wall that he and the farm's owner had built together and walked through the fence he had mended, up to the door.

After a breath, Goblin Slayer stood before the old wooden door, but did not immediately make to open it. First, he dug in the pouch of items at his waist, pulling out a bag that bulged with gold coins. It had a good heft in his hand. He loosened the strings and checked the contents. Everything was in order. He put it away. His steel helmet moved right, then left. Finally, he lifted his gaze to the sky.

"Good," he whispered faintly, then put his hand on the doorknob. He turned it and pushed the door open.

Along with the creaking of the door came a relaxing warmth and a sweet aroma. Just as he registered that it was something boiled with milk, the girl standing in the kitchen turned around.

"Phew! You were out late today." She blinked in surprise, wiping her hands on her apron and hurrying around the kitchen.

He closed the door behind him, entering the house with studied steps. She glanced at him and saw the basket he carried at his side.

"What's with the corn? Looks great!"

"A gift," he said, placing the basket on the table.

"Oh yeah?" she said, stirring the large pot. Without looking at him, she added, "Not on top of the table."

"Hrk."

"At least put it on a chair."

"Where's your uncle?"

"He said he had a meeting today. He'll be late."

"Very well, then." He pulled out a chair with a clatter and set the basket on it. The bundle of corn sat there proudly as if it were the guest of honor. He gave a grunt and nodded.

In the meantime, she had been scurrying all over the kitchen. "Just a moment, okay? It'll be ready soon."

"All right," he said. He went over to his chair, placing his hand on the back.

"Hm?" She glanced over her shoulder when he showed no sign of sitting down as he usually did. She found him standing next to the chair, silent.

Hmm… Drying her hands on her apron, she left the fire and pattered up to his side. *It's usually best for me to coax it out of him when he gets like this.*

"What's up?" She leaned forward, as if trying to glimpse his face under his helmet.

That familiar helmet. It hid his expression, and yet, she had a good sense of what was under it now.

"Mm." He was silent for a moment before finally saying, "Nothing." After another moment, he said, "Before we eat—"

"Yes?"

"—there's something I want to give you."

Bit by bit the words left his mouth, and then he rifled through his item pouch. He produced the bag of gold coins he had been checking earlier. It jangled as he set it on the table.

She blinked, surprised. "What's this? I thought you already paid this month's rent."

"It is not rent." He spoke even more bluntly than usual. "Happy birthday."

"Oh!" She clapped her hands. He was right. She had been so busy, she'd completely forgotten about it.

Tomorrow is my nineteenth birthday.

"I didn't know what to get you, so I thought this would be best," he said, pushing the bag toward her. It might have been more trouble than it was worth to wrap it, but even so, it was in an exceptionally ordinary, undecorated leather pouch. And it was full of *money.* As a birthday present, it didn't rank very high.

"You know, you…" A number of expressions passed over Cow Girl's face, all difficult to read. Should she be angry? Or upset? Or annoyed, or sad? Finally she settled on a bemused smile. "…are hopeless."

She hugged the pouch of gold coins to her chest the way a child might a new doll.

"You act like you don't know anything, and then just when I think maybe you do know a thing or two…it turns out you really don't know anything."

"Erk…"

"If you're not sure what to get, take me along. We can choose something together."

That's what I really want.

He grunted softly at her words, then nodded his helmet up and down slowly. "…I understand."

"That answer doesn't inspire confidence. I'll thank you…once we've chosen my gift." She giggled, realizing she was lecturing him, and patted him on the back. "I've got high hopes for the harvest festival, okay?" She was smiling. She didn't sound like she was expecting much at all.

So she didn't take him too seriously when he said, "I will think about it."

"Sure, sure. Anyway, sit down. Dinner's ready—let's eat!"

Then she placed her hands on his shoulders, made broad by his armor, and guided him into the chair. She headed back to the kitchen, but turned around as a thought crossed her mind.

"Oh, yeah, I forgot something important." She made sure to give him the brightest smile she could. "Welcome home!"

"Thanks," he nodded, quietly shifting in his chair. "I'm back."

AFTERWORD

Hullo, Kumo Kagyu here. Did you all enjoy Volume 4?

I designed this volume as a collection of short stories, mostly taking place either between Volumes 1 and 2 or Volumes 2 and 3. They're stories in which a number of different people think and do a number of different things, and a variety of different things happen. That meant fewer goblins than usual, but there was still a little bit of goblin slaying in this book.

There's also a limited edition of Volume 4 that includes a drama CD. It depicts an adventure involving Priestess and High Elf Archer, so not too many goblins there, either. But don't fret; I did work in at least one goblin-slaying scene. And I'm so impressed with the actresses. I was completely surprised. It left me thinking I should have had this or that character show up, or just put in more lines altogether… Thoughts like those made me keep my head down as I listened to the recording. I'm told other authors are the same way. It's not just me!

Plus, *Goblin Slayer* took top prize for a new series in the "This Light Novel is Awesome!" contest! I can't tell you how pleased I am, but… are they sure they want such a weird book getting first place? It's just the story of an adventurer who talks about nothing but goblins and slays nothing but goblins.

In any event, there will be plenty more goblins, and you can rest assured that "Mr. GobSlay" will slay them. Volume 5 will be set immediately after Volume 3 and feature goblins who live on a snowy mountain and have to be slain.

Volume 1 featured a hill, Volume 2 took place underneath a city, Volume 3 featured a seven-armed monster, Volume 4 was a bye, and Volume 5 will be a mountain fortress. Some of you may already see where I'm going with this. But if you don't, don't worry. Either way, I'm so happy everyone is enjoying the adventures of my strange little adventurer. Please stick around for the ride.

Thanks to Mr. Kannatuki for yet another volume of wonderful illustrations. Padfoot Waitress actually came out of his pictures.

Mr. Kurose, I eagerly await your manga version each month, and I can't wait to see more of it.

Thank you to the actors who participated in the drama CD; your performances are wonderful.

Thanks as always to my gaming buddies and the other creative types in my life.

To all the editorial staff, and everyone involved in the production, promotion, and distribution of this book, I owe you so much.

To all my readers and my site administrator, you are the reason I've made it this far.

I'll continue to give this series my all—I hope you'll come with me!

HE DOES NOT LET ANYONE ROLL THE DICE.

A young Priestess joins her first adventuring party, but blind to the dangers, they almost immediately find themselves in trouble. It's Goblin Slayer who comes to their rescue—a man who has dedicated his life to the extermination of all goblins by any means necessary. A dangerous, dirty, and thankless job, but he does it better than anyone. And when rumors of his feats begin to circulate, there's no telling who might come calling next...

Light Novel V.1-2 Available Now!

Check out the simul-pub manga chapters every month!

www.yenpress.com